THE FIFTH PASSENGER

AND OTHER PERVERSITIES

Scott R.S. Raphael

Dedicated to

Granddad and Kathy

Table of Contents

Author's Note

The following is a collection of short stories that I wrote from about 2016 to 2022. A lot changed during that time, both personally and in terms of my writing style. When I started the earliest of these entries, I was still in university, studying English, and trying to emulate the brilliance of some of the masters.

By the latest end of that period, I was tired of not being able to understand half of what I was writing upon reread.

Don't worry. Those days are long gone and (I think/hope) everything makes sense in this collection.

When I decided to put this book together, I rounded up all the darker short stories that I'd written and carelessly planned to include them all. Naturally, that did not happen. Some just weren't ready, others needed a re-write. Some needed more than *just* a re-write. And others just didn't fit the mood.

As a result, I separated a few stories into different thematic categories and prepared two-plus collections for your reading pleasure (hopefully).

I needed to publish this collection first because this was the one that was always meant to come first. As soon as I wrote "The Fifth Passenger", I knew that it was a title story, and I knew that the subtitle would be "and Other Perversities". A file by that name has been sitting on my computer for a long time with just one file contained therein.

Now, it is a reality.

So what, exactly, constituted a perversity for the purposes of this book? There's a lot of room to manoeuvre within that word and, as I've discovered through my explorations of how far I'm willing to push boundaries (it's quite far), almost anything can be made perverse if looked at from the right angle. Some of the works that didn't make it into this collection are perverse, as well. They just fit better elsewhere.

The stories that *did* make it into this collection follow principally (although, not exclusively) one element of the perverse: the uncannily real; the uncomfortably possible. Some explore the supernatural. Some, the purely natural. Many, somewhere in between.

Because no life goes completely untouched by the unexplained and unexplainable. And no life goes untouched by the explainable that, nonetheless, one really doesn't want to explain.

In the end, the main goal of these stories isn't always to make the reader uncomfortable, but it's definitely one of the goals. That's what I enjoy and that's what I intend to subject you to, as a result. If these tales make you feel unwell, dirty, shaky, sick, or afraid to turn out the lights, then they've done their job. But if only just make you think or wonder, just a little, about sides of life that you wouldn't normally consider, then they've succeeded, as well.

Welcome to an exploration of my dreams and fears. To unpleasant realities.

To the perversities that should never have been written.

~ Scott R.S. Raphael

THE FIFTH PASSENGER

AND OTHER PERVERSITIES

What Hearts Are Meant to Do

This is not my home, nor my love, but I shall adopt them both until I am otherwise obliged. And I fear that, soon, that obligation will fall and I will be callously compelled to execute my task and my morality in a moment of tragic unpersoning, wherein I will be neither myself nor not myself, and where, although the former will be my preference, the latter will never leave.

But, for now, I am busy; busy neglecting the cardinal rule of my instructors and guides. When is the moment that a self-told lie becomes true? When does a thought cease to be but a thought and become an ever-ingrained fact of a body's very function? I fear that I have crossed that threshold and have become a new self that I had specifically intended to dispel. Somewhere within, Troy has been taken, and I know not whether I am the Trojans, the Greeks, or the horse.

The television is on—some program about quolls—and I struggle to believe that either of us is conscious of it. Though, what of her mind? Haven't I been warned? Haven't I seen? Her neck turns and draws the scratching fibres of my shirt across my chest before her chin drives into my fourth rib. Her viridian eyes are upturned and I can feel their smooth questioning without a glance. It is between mechanic and desire that my hand creeps tenderly to the back of her head and strokes her long, wavy, blonde hair, as though carefully surveying the edge of a lately shattered mirror.

Am I meant to feel this hum, as of melting wax dripping beneath my bones? Or, if I may rephrase, am I meant to feel it *at this juncture*? And how does it justify itself in conjunction with the splattering bacon grease presently caking my brain? Perhaps needless to say, I am confused.

She wants me to kiss her, I know, and I do, my eyes crawling through the dark across the photographs of her last boyfriend, her marble figurines, her freshly framed degree. The kiss ends and she stands wordlessly. She's nearly as tall as I am. At times, my distorted imagination envisions her at equal height, or greater, and I don't know why, or why she's present at all outside of my demanded designs.

The bathroom door closes with a click and I rise to examine more closely the artifacts of my previous interest. But I retreat on my heart's palpitating warning. Or upon the silent but unavoidable buzzing from my pocket that issues the night's edict. I quell the alarm, but not mine.

How did I get this far? I could have failed at any time. I could have ensured it. I could have done it without drawing attention. But what would follow? I had no desire to consider that future. There would be no curtailing this end, so is it not for the best that it is me?

Her return is shorter than her parting, as I catch a mere glimpse of her upper thigh before she is ingested by the darkness of the bedroom. I strip there and follow.

I run a Latexed finger along her beautiful body as my eyes struggle to focus. I pound my chest; I caress hers. I feel the gurgling thud in my throat. I drive my sullied hand into the gurgling sludge that separates lifeline from life. And I squeeze. I squeeze the limp, dead organ. But, at once, every semblance of life and love and hate and desire and passion and anger and confusion and reality and fantasy and death crumble beneath my fingertips as my frozen brain registers the fact of the moment.

This is not what hearts are meant to do.

Reclothed, yet colder than before, I find myself outside in an unfamiliar neighbourhood. This is not my home nor my love, but it is my path and my achievement. And they will be pleased by my success. And each step that I take back to where I began echoes with a familiar th-thump-th-thump-th-thump.

Figures of Tomorrow

The driveway was covered in stone pellets, and firs obscured the vision around the bend, but for all of its distance and secrecy, the trio of wanderers did not expect a mansion on the other end.

"Daaaaamnnnnn," Max whistled, lazily flicking his cigarette off the main path, barely sweeping past an awestruck Robbie, too engrossed in the fantastic sight to notice his brush with the third degree.

As his co-workers—friends?—reacted, Corbin slid to the front of the pack, a familiar position adopted from his years of bossing the other two around—in the most congenial manner possible, though both were generally incompetent at their jobs—and regarded the sight in full.

The house was grand, indeed. Grand enough to warrant both reactions behind him. But Corbin was not so uncouth as Max, nor so immovable as Robbie. Surely, it was one of the nicer homes he'd encountered, but he was not to be deterred by majesty. After all, growing up in rural Alabama, his father had owned acres upon acres of land, spread like the rings of a dartboard around the sprawling three-storey estate he had grown up in. He was glad to be away from there.

"Come on, we're late," Corbin quickened his pace, although he had no real desire to reach those wide, oak double-doors, nor much care for what lay behind the pillared façade. He was a little chilly.

The night had taken a turn and a breeze was crack-
ling the late autumn leaves as it lifted the ridges in
their skin, but even this was not his principal reason
for hurrying.

If he was honest with himself, he just wanted to
get the night over with. And it was hard to imagine
that the others weren't feeling much the same.

When Gerrit had shown up at Lemming-Gray,
Inc., he had seemed much like the other fly-by-night
managers who'd tickled the edges of the corporation
before delivering a resounding 'nope' that was followed by a hasty resignation. And who could
blame them? Corbin chuckled softly to himself as
he thought about the promotion he'd been offered
six months ago—declined. No, he'd lead from
within, but God forbid he take any of the actual responsibility.

The financials were in the toilet, the organiza-
tional structure was drawn in crayon by a third
grader, and the survival of the company rested principally upon the strings of a violist who'd long ago
forgotten to tune his instrument. They stayed afloat
on good fortune, history, and the continued patron-
age of an anonymous client who probably just
didn't want the world to know that it got its décor
from such a disreputable company.

No, Corbin had always aspired higher than the
limits of a simple salesman, but the money was regular, the day ended at five, and no one ever blamed
him for the scandals. And it got him out of Butler
County.

But then Gerrit had arrived and the entire atmosphere of LGI had changed. Not necessarily for the better, but when it was hard to change for the worse, different could not be taken lightly.

Sales went up. Scandals went down. Reputability…well, it didn't get worse, anyway.

And it didn't stop at the atmosphere beyond the scope of the office. Within the daily confines of white walls, carpeted dividers, and plastic screens, something was different.

The building had energy like it had never had before. Gerrit was a wildcard, a joker. He could walk in and change the energy of the room without a word. From the moment he arrived, it was obvious that he wasn't going to be like the rest. No fear of the evils associated with a tarnished brand. No desire to walk away from a fight. But, also, seemingly no concept that any of these issues were issues, at all.

Gerrit floated through the days with a wonky, lopsided smile on his face, a half-shaved beard that was so consistently wrong that it almost had to be intentional, and permanently bleary eyes that looked like they were either always on the brink of tears or ready to burst from his head at the lightest of touches.

For six weeks, they saw the man, heard of his success, even said 'hi' to him in the halls. But not once did they feel like they knew the curious figure behind door 163 (they never re-labelled the doors, ready to change leaders at a moment's notice).

Finally, he just faded into the background like everything else—a figure of prominence in a place that didn't matter once the clock struck home. And that was the moment he chose to strike. "Corbin Bates, Max Server, and Robbie Rayfield?" he'd called out in a twittering voice that did not match with his six-foot-nine stature, looking at each of them directly though they had no clue how he'd known their names. And that was the first time, they realized, that anyone had heard him speak. "I want to take you to dinner. Now. Let's go."

And at two-thirty in the afternoon, the group of long-serving salesmen had gone to the most curious 'dinner' they'd ever experienced, watching Gerrit Colfax consume dessert as an appetizer, a pitcher of spicy margarita, and the entirety of a finish-it-in-forty-five-minutes-or-less-and-it's-free pork platter (in thirty-four minutes, no less). And all of this without a single word spoken.

Then, as he was paying the bill for the table, Gerrit declared, "This was the loveliest experience I've had in ages. We should do this again!"

And so they did. Sometimes at a more reasonable dinner hour, sometimes earlier. By week four, the men were ignoring phone calls in the dead of night to avoid strip clubs and twenty-four-hour diners. But so little was said, so little was understood.

"He's just trying to make friends," Corbin had justified, and Robbie had nodded ferociously in assent.

"But he's a freak," Max had contested, and Robbie had, again, nodded furiously.

And though Corbin may not have wished to attend, Max may actively have detested the concept, and Robbie may not have understood how to decline, all felt impelled to comply with the various idiosyncrasies and curiosities of their new manager's whims. Which, at the very least, brought the three of them closer together.

And now, on the precipice of Gerrit's doorstep, they felt drawn forth by the unusual aura of their superior—still looking forward to going home at the end of the night, but unable to resist the pull of the man who'd paid for so many of their expensive meals. He had invited them to his home to meet his wife and to solidify their burgeoning bond. And, if nothing else, they were all curious to find out who would marry such a curious figure.

"Maybe we should ask if we can hang out on this patio," Robbie offered as uselessly as he did most of his at-work suggestions, as though the weather weren't threatening to dip below freezing. "It's a real nice patio."

"Or," Max offered, lighting up a joint and taking two quick puffs before butting out the rest for later, "you could sit out here while we…" coughing fit, "sit inside" coughing fit.

For a moment, it seemed Robbie might actually have been considering it, but an owl in the distance combined with a creak from Corbin's step along the well-manicured but structurally unsettling wood floor panels snapped him out of it. "I'm good."

Corbin raised his hand to rap, but something drew his fingers to the brass lion's head knocker in the centre of the right door—lonely, with its left door partner lost to nature, a vague outline still visible, even in the dark of night.

Thud, thud, thud.

So dull it seemed that it may not even have been heard.

But, a moment later, the host, himself, had thrust the door open, arms flung wide to greet his 'friends' into his bathrobed embrace. "My boys!" he declared in his flutter of a voice from his perch on high shoulders. "Enter, please." He pulled the pipe from his crooked mouth, which had bounded up and down as he'd spoken.

All seemed to be waiting for another to guide him beyond the threshold, but it was Corbin who—to no one's surprise—ended up taking the lead.

"This is a really nice place, you've got," Corbin offered as Max, behind Gerrit's back, made a crude symbol of 'suck up.'

"Hm," Gerrit mused. "For now." He led them through the grand front hall, past an evergreen stone winding staircase and a marble bust of Lincoln.

"Planning on moving?"

"Wherever the wind may blow, eh, boys?"

Corbin wasn't sure how he felt about being called a 'boy,' even with the most endearing of intentions. Max was quite sure and grimaced every time he heard the word. Robbie didn't notice.

A quick left turn led them to a spacious sitting room, lined with closed doors that, if opened, could only have made this grand space seem like a house unto itself. Despite the massive appearance of the place, it was weakly furnished, with little more than a few paintings—some of which seemed to be prints—the occasional empty plinth, and a three-cushioned couch in the centre of the room, set directly before an armchair. If nothing else, the paltry décor spoke to how rarely this sitting room saw use.

Gerrit energetically gestured to the couch and his three employees shuffled their way to seated positions, exchanging side-glances all the while. "I think I'll stand," Max muttered but, in the echoing chamber, he couldn't bring himself to say it with force, or to act upon it.

Squeezed into the middle of the sofa, Corbin did his best not to splay out upon Robbie to his left or Max to his right, while Gerrit stood awkwardly before them, waxing poetic about the glories of the room. "This is my Uncle Eldridge," he indicated a dark, abstract painting, "and Aunt Matilda is over the fireplace—" a ghostly white and featureless figure on a sickly beige background. He leaned in conspiratorially, "—have to keep her warm."

"Definitely doesn't look too hot to me," Max muttered and Corbin elbowed him.

"But what *am* I doing?!" Gerrit perked up at a moment's inspiration. "I still haven't introduced you to my wife!" Bursting quickly through a door behind his hard-backed armchair, he disappeared into the darkness for a moment and, before the three men could exchange glances of confusion, their host had returned, arms awkwardly positioned at his side and something hidden just behind his back.

Corbin, Max, and Robbie, standing politely, craned their necks to get a look at the hidden surprise, wondering at the lack of a second human before them and trying to figure out if she was still coming, or if she'd hidden so perfectly behind her husband that even her legs were entirely blocked from view.

As Gerrit reached the armchair again, he whipped his arms out from behind his back and his employees were faced with a cold, white porcelain doll. "I'd like you to meet my wife, Serena."

As if of its own accord, the doll's head turned toward them, its flat blue eyes staring blankly, both at nothing and straight through their chests. Its hands hung limply at its sides and its legs lolled toward the floor. She was clad in a turquoise frock and black Mary Janes. Everything about her screamed 1950s. Everything about her screamed old, cold, and dead. Her face was scratched on the left cheek, a finger was missing from her right hand. But her hair—her soft, luscious blonde hair. That was alive, flowing down her back and over her shoulders. Her hair drew them in.

The trio stared at the figure for a moment, trying to grasp its significance—because, surely, Gerrit could not have meant—but *really!*

As their eyes slowly crept back to Gerrit's unnervingly gleeful smile, the already cold night became a touch colder. "Say hi, honey!" The corners of his lips crept ever further up his face as he looked back to the men. "She's shy."

Max was going to say something, Corbin could feel it. And fearing what that might be, the leader of the troupe swallowed drily and offered the first, "Hello, Mrs. Colfax. It's so nice to meet you." His hand spasmed—should he reach out to shake?

"Hi," Robbie chirped, but the air had left his body and the 'i' didn't quite make it past his lips.

Max hesitated for a moment, looking his coworkers up and down and gauging the situation before turning to Gerrit and smirking, "Man, what a doll!"

The doll's—Serena's—*its* hands shifted to cover its—her—mouth. Gerrit smiled proudly, "Aw, you've made her bashful. It's okay, sweetie, he's just being friendly." The hand lowered. "Come, let's sit!" And Gerrit took the lead to the armchair.

Max flung himself down on the couch, spreading out a bit more, now, and somehow enjoying the atmosphere, a wide grin forming on his face. Corbin followed him to sit, while Robbie stayed upright until a gentle tap on the knee from Corbin brought him back down.

"So, how long have you, um, been together?" Corbin ventured, the final word cracking in his throat.

"Oh, years now," Gerrit waved his free hand casually. "We met in…'91, was it?" he looked to the doll for reassurance. She made no move.

"That's a—that's a long time. Definitely something to aspire to."

"What's that, honey?" Gerrit stared into the cold, dead blue eyes of his porcelain princess. The doll's hands rose once more, cupping Gerrit's ear as her body shifted, ever-so-slightly, forward. "Mm, oh, she says it's lovely to meet you all and she's heard so much about you. And—honey!" he looked sternly upon the figure and tsked. "She says you're much nicer than I said; can you believe that?"

"People've said crazier things," Max mused wryly and Corbin shot him a quick elbow when Gerrit wasn't looking.

"How about you, Robbie?" Gerrit whipped quickly in his direction and Robbie fell further into his cushion. "Why don't you tell Serena all about what it's like to work in the décor industry?"

Robbie opened his mouth, but no sound came out. And each time his lips parted and closed, parted and closed, the doll's head turned just a few millimetres more, facing him, inching closer and closer across Gerrit's knee. "I—ah—we—ah…"

"Or maybe you, Corbin?" Gerrit turned upon the middleman, teeth bared sharply in what could conceivably have been called a grin. "What's it like, working for silly old me?"

"It's an honour, sir. The company—it's an escape, really. A home away from home."

From deep within Gerrit's throat, a low, animal croak pronounced, "Kiss-ass."

"Honey!" Gerrit's normal, twittering tone returned, along with a look of shock. "We're in polite company," he murmured in the doll's ear. "I do apologize. Serena's not used to company. But she really does like you all."

"Oh, no, not at all," Corbin attempted to recover, but his heart had chilled at the sound of the horrible voice that came from Gerrit's throat. "It truly is a pleasure…"

He was interrupted by a resounding ding, echoing from beyond the hall, as if the whole house had been shaken by it, though it pealed in such a short, small tone. "That must be the snacks!" Gerrit declared. "Just a little finger food, nothing special, but Serena's been working on it *just* for you!" He smiled at each in turn, that sharp, biting smile, the doll's head following his but much more slowly. "We'll be right back."

The door to the grand hall shut behind him and swept, with it, all the air from the room.

Robbie gasped loudly, screeching for air and trying, somehow, to formulate a thought into a word. "What. The. Hell…"

"Shh!" Corbin chided, heart racing, eyes darting, but unable to move from his seated position. "There's probably a reasonable explanation…"

"There is: he's psycho," Max lazed deeper into the couch and drummed his fingers along the arm-rest. "But we knew that already."

"You don't think," Robbie finally managed to find words. "The doll, it wasn't…?"

"No. He must have been moving it somehow," Corbin shook his head firmly, though he wasn't entirely confident, himself.

"Noooo," Max shook his head sarcastically, "you mean the plastic friggin' doll isn't alive?"

"Porcelain," Robbie choked out, not fully realizing he was doing it. Corbin reached forward to put a hand on the pale man's shoulder and found that, even through his shirt, he was cold.

"Sit back. Relax. We're all here," he soothed. "In a few hours, it'll be over and you can turn in your notice on Monday." But Robbie's eyes were locked upon the shut and bolted window. Locked upon the dark shadows of empty tree branches that slipped along the salmon-coloured carpet, creeping upon them like fingers of the damned.

With a gust of frigid air, the door to the hall burst open with a clatter and Gerrit entered triumphantly, foot still in the air from where his wispy-yet-massive frame had thrust all its weight into the door. Meanwhile, his hands were occupied with a cloche-covered tray and a mistress of Hell.

"Who wants an *amuse-bouche*?"

Max's hand shot up in the air as Gerrit manoeuvred the pinky finger of his doll hand to raise the cloche and reveal a tray of steaming, toothpicked octopus tentacle bites beside an ambiguous red dip. *It's seafood sauce*, Corbin told himself but, aloud, he whispered to Max, "Don't you *dare* touch those things."

"They're still a little hot," Gerrit cautioned.

Deflating, Max shook his head—mostly at Corbin, but as far as Gerrit was concerned, for the situation—"Guess I'll have to wait."

"They're Serena's favourite," Gerrit noted, setting the tray down on his seat as he fished a TV tray out from a side door before setting the meal atop it. "I never did care for them, though."

"They look amazing. I really wish I weren't allergic to seafood," Corbin mimed sadness, he thought, effectively.

"Oh, I'm so sorry," Gerrit retook his seat, "I didn't think to ask. I was sure you'd had the seabass the last time we went to The Captain's." The doll's head turned slowly to face him, in judgement.

"I, um," Corbin's mouth dried once more, "I think that must've been Robbie," but Robbie was shaking his head vigorously, "or Max." Max just shrugged.

"No matter," Gerrit stroked his wife's hair as he watched Corbin from the corner of his eye. "While we wait for these to cool, would anyone be up for a game?"

And, for the first time that night, even Max hesitated. "What kind of game?" he ventured slowly.

"Oh, I don't know. Serena, what do you think?" he leaned in close to hear the doll's opinion. "Mm, yes. That's a nice one, isn't it? You're always thinking of such nice things. Okay," he turned his voice back to the 'boys.' "Serena would like to play a game called Compliments, where we each say one nice thing about another player."

Collectively, the others inwardly sighed with relief. Aside from Robbie, who, still, could not breathe.

"I'll go first," Gerrit began. "Corbin, I like your work ethic."

"Thank you, sir."

"Kiss-ass!" came the guttural animal voice.

"I'm sorry!" Gerrit appeared flustered. "Serena's just having a joke. It's her way. But I forgot to explain all of the rules. If you say 'thank you,' you lose. This is a game about giving, not receiving. That's what friends do, after all, isn't it?" He waited for a reply, but received little more than a half-nod from Corbin and a small titter from Max. "But, we'll start again. Okay: Corbin, I like your hair."

Instinctively, Corbin ran his hand along his short, well-kept black hair, opening his mouth but quickly catching himself and closing it again.

"Okay, Serena, it's your turn." The doll's head turned once more, flat eyes glazing over each member of the room, everyone hoping not to be seen. And then she whispered in Gerrit's ear—

No! Corbin screamed inwardly. *She's not whispering. He's just a deranged fool with a doll. Nothing more.*

"Oh. Oh!" Gerrit smiled mischievously. "Well, I can't repeat that out loud in polite company but, suffice it to say, her compliment was for yours truly. Robbie, you're up."

"P-pass…"

"Come now, Robbie! It's all in good fun. Or do you have nothing nice to say about any of us? That wouldn't be the case, would it?" Gerrit leaned forward and Robbie's breathing quickened.

"No, no. I—I like Max's sense of humour."

"Good one, good one!" Gerrit declared.

Max weighed saying 'thank you' and self-eliminating but, after a moment's thought, reconsidered.

"Robbie, I like your inner strength," Corbin offered, looking hard at his seatmate, trying to stare him into settling down, but Robbie was still recovering from the previous moment and didn't notice.

"All right, Max. On to you," Gerrit smiled, as if he knew what was coming, but Max ploughed through, anyway.

"Serena," Max grinned, and Corbin snapped his neck around in horror. "I love your skin. It's like…porcelain."

Gerrit just stared at Max, eyes transfixed, leering, leering. And so, too, did the doll, now immobile

but seeming to inch ever closer in its stasis. No one
said a word. No one breathed.

"A very astute observation," Gerrit noted, stroking his wife's hair again. "Very astute, indeed.
Well," he snapped back to the rest of the room,
"enough of that. Good fun and all, but it's time to
eat."

"Ladies first," Max offered, apparently unfazed.

"No, no—please! Guests first."

"I wouldn't feel right…" but Max was shot down
with a glare. Now, for the first time uncomfortable,
he felt drawn to the metal tray that Gerrit raised and
extended. "Thank you, sir. Serena." He plucked
the least curled of the tentacles from the batch and
held it gingerly between his thumb and forefinger,
eyeing it as a prospector might pyrite. The tray
glided past Corbin, bobbing threateningly close
along its arc, slicing past his neck.

And then it was before Robbie; he stared at it
blankly, as though he was unfamiliar with the concept of food. Gerrit shifted the tray upward, silently
compelling the inevitable. Jaw clenched, eyes still
darting to the window, the creeping fingers of free-
dom imprisoned behind a padlock—a *padlock!*—
Robbie sensed no alternative. And it was thus that
he lunged forward and speared the pad of his index
finger with a toothpick, barely registering the pain
as he shoveled the coarse suction cups into his
mouth and swallowed without chewing.

Everyone stared at him wordlessly for a moment,
and then Gerrit turned back to his wife—his doll—

his *beast*. "Ready, Shnookums?" Gerrit raised a tentacle and twirled it between his fingers, gaze locked upon the blank blue eyes that stared over his shoulder, seeing the whole room out of the corner of its eye.

Slowly, as a parent to a child, Gerrit lowered the hors d'oeuvre toward the unparting porcelain lips. Closer, closer—he made no reaction, no acknowledgement that they would not open for him. As though—he thought that they were already parted.

Even Max was struck by the perversity, the impossibility. Closer, the tentacle moved and, repulsed, closer moved the trio of onlookers, as well.

And just as the curled tip was threatening to tickle her lip, Gerrit stopped, frozen in time. His eyes peeled aside to watch the other three and no one moved. Then, the corner of his lip turned upward and, a moment later, he was convulsing in a full-on laugh. A bellowing, painful laugh that matched his monstrous height but fell far away from his usual, twittering voice.

And as Max, Corbin, and Robbie backed away in their seats, barely realizing they were doing so, he only laughed harder, gasping, panting, sucking in what little air was left in the room and expelling it back out in violence.

But as instantly as this fit had begun, it had ceased, Gerrit looking upon his underlings deviously, his mirth transmogrified into a sinister smirk. "You. *Actually*. Believed it. Didn't you?"

No one spoke. They exchanged glances without a motion of the head, but no one wanted to break the silence.

"Did you really think I was so mad—so absolutely *bonkers*—as to think I was married to a porcelain doll?"

Slowly, the men began to chuckle nervously, Corbin first, and the others following his lead.

"Come on, boys! She was moving on her own! You didn't think that was the least bit suspicious?" The doll moved left to right in his hand, head snapping back and forth. Gerrit lifted the base of the dress and revealed the wires beneath. "And I thought I had the brightest minds in the business on my team! Ha!"

"You—" Corbin began, trying to recapture his breath as he forced the words out, stomach still tense enough to buckle him, though he fought the sensation. "You're just one step ahead of us."

"Kiss-ass!" Gerrit declared in his animal voice but, this time, with a note of humour. He turned to Max, "And you—taking advantage of a poor madman with your jokes! You should be ashamed," though he said it with a grin.

"Well, I mean…I never believed it for a second," Max attempted feebly.

Gerrit shook his head. "I've always wanted to try that, but I *really* never thought it would work so well. A doll, my goodness. Who would have thought that a *doll* could cause so much concern?"

His body warming slightly, Corbin attempted to distract himself with speech, with a return to the normalcy and comfort of a regular conversation, "I guess we really just didn't know what to expect. I mean, you invite us over to meet your wife and then you're so convincing. I'm assuming we're not *actually* going to be meeting your wife, then?"

"Oh, but boys," Gerrit said seriously, "you already have." Collectively, they hesitated. "No, no, not like that! We've moved past that joke. But Serena really *is* my wife. In a way." Gerrit stroked the doll's hair once more and looked upon it fondly. "You see, my wife—Serena—she died, tragically, a few years ago. Very unexpected. An accident. And I just couldn't bear to let her go, so I had this doll made to look exactly like her." He ran his finger slowly down the doll's face, across its raised cheekbones and under its pointed chin. "It really *is* a true likeness. Sometimes, when I've just woken up from a dream, I really *do* think she's…come back to me." He sighed, then shook his head and went silent.

"I'm very sorry," Corbin offered, unsure of whether he should approach and console the man, but Gerrit was already waving him away.

"It was a long time ago, but some things—they never go away. It gets…lonely. That's why I'm glad to have good friends, like you. You keep me sane. Grounded." He looked up at them again, a small twinkle in his eye, "And I *am* sane; I promise."

"She's a very beautiful representation," Corbin offered.

"Indeed," Gerrit appreciated the compliment more than he could have any for himself. "It's her real hair, you know," he stroked the doll's head gently. "It took a long time to clean out all of the…but never mind that. I'm just glad to have something of her left."

With that, Gerrit rose. "You can eat that, by the way," he gestured to the toothpick still hanging loosely from Max's fingers. "It's not poisoned. And your mouth's all ready for it anyway," he noted, indicating Max's jaw, which still hung slightly open from the recent revelations.

Quickly, Gerrit returned to the side door and set the doll in the room it had come from before returning. "I'll have dinner ready soon. It's seabass— and, Corbin, you can stop pretending you're allergic to seafood now."

Corbin chuckled drily, embarrassed.

"Now, where were we?" Gerrit returned to his armchair. But, before he could sit, a chime sounded in his pocket. Checking his cellphone, he shook his head solemnly. "Sorry, boys. Looks like I'm going to have to take this outside. Feel free to stretch your legs. I'll bring in some more chairs when I come back." He answered the call. "Hello?"

And with that, he disappeared from the room.

For a moment, no one said anything, Max running a hand through his long, dirty blonde hair, trying to think of a way to pretend he hadn't had a moment of fear; Robbie, eyes closed, doing breathing exercises; and Corbin, slumping so far down on the couch that his back was lying and his lower half was overhanging the ground.

Finally, Max broke the silence. "So…you realize we're all major idiots, right?"

"It was…really convincing," Robbie pronounced each word slowly, carefully.

"This is why we shouldn't go about making assumptions and jumping to conclusions…"

But Max cut Corbin off, "Oh, come on, man. You were just as bad as him, just louder about it."

"I don't know if *that's* fair," Corbin contested.

"Hey! Cut me some slack," Robbie was only pretending to be upset, but it was hard for him to differentiate between pretend and real at that moment.

"Maybe I went a *little* too far, there," Max admitted, needling Robbie a little further before jumping to his feet. "You were much worse," he skipped over to the nearly-recovered man and tousled his mid-length chestnut hair.

"Hey!"

"I actually did want to try one of these," Max chucked two tentacles into his mouth at once and chewed quickly. He shrugged, "Needs lemon."

"Not a big fan of lemon," Corbin took one, himself, and played with the gelatinous texture between his back molars. "Could do with some salt, though. What are you doing?" Corbin looked up to see Max

strolling casually to the side door where the doll
was kept.

"I wanna take another look at that doll," he
turned the handle lazily and threw the door open
like he owned the place.

"Don't do that. It's not our place."

"Hey, you're not my boss, here." Max thought
for a second. "And you're not my boss at work, either, even though you act like it. So, chill out and
let me do my thing."

Seeing no point in arguing, Corbin turned to
Robbie. "How you doing?"

He shrugged, bouncing his head one way, then
the other. "Could do with some fresh air, but I'll
live."

"I'm sure Gerrit wouldn't mind if we opened a
window…"

"Good luck," Robbie gestured over to the creeping shadows. "Padlocked."

Corbin chewed his cheek, "Kind of weird. Guess
he doesn't want anyone getting in."

"Guys?"

Corbin and Robbie both turned to face the side
room, where Max had disappeared into the darkness. "What's going on?"

"Um, uh, I don't…" Max sputtered.

In unison, Corbin and Robbie jumped up and
headed for the room, nearly colliding as they entered at the same time. "What is it?"

The room was in darkness, with just a tiny sliver
of moonlight cutting through the high, padlocked

window near the ceiling. Max had his cellphone flashlight on, aimed straight at the Serena doll, its face morphed in the shadows. Cruel. Sinister.

"It's just the doll…" Corbin began, half-expecting to see the thing move of its own accord. But Max was shaking his head; they could just tell in the black. Hesitantly, shakingly, he moved his hand to the opposite side of the room, across a wooden chair, a set of metal table legs, and a scratched and worn teak desk. On top of that desk sat three shadowy figures.

Even with the flashlight, it was dark—too dark to see every detailed feature. But there was no denying what they were.

One doll that looked exactly like Robbie.

One doll that looked exactly like Max.

One doll that looked exactly like Corbin.

All designed perfectly down to the last feature, last blemish, last birthmark.

Except for the hair. All three dolls were bareheaded. Waiting to be crowned.

"It was good having you over," came a soft, twittering voice from the doorframe behind them. Slowly, they each turned to face Gerrit, towering miles above them in the darkness, the moonlight glinting off the razor clutched tightly in his hand. "It's been so nice to have the company." He raised his hand and the blade was lost in the black.

"I hope you weren't planning on leaving."

Changing Storefronts

It might be a touch self-aggrandizing to say that I am an important man, but I also think it would be a touch self-diminishing to say otherwise. I'm well-respected in business, trustworthy, and afforded a place at the peak of society. Furthermore, I'm desirable, in every sense of the word. I don't mean to sound the narcissist. Indeed, I have no particular interest in myself at all. It merely seems important to note, if I'm to provide an accurate picture of what it's like to be *me*, that these things are true.

But what are claims without examples and justifications? Everything must be defined with essay-like clarity in life, or else it will go challenged and derided.

First, to justify my importance, I would point to my job. Maybe, some would argue, our occupations are not our lives and shouldn't be our primary, defining feature. But for someone who spends so much of his time hard at work, in an office that he's earned through years of torturous toiling, I think it's fair to say that, in my case at any rate, my profession is very much me. *I* am a CEO. *Chief* Executive Officer. *Chief*. First, principal, main. That's me. So, I think it goes without further saying that, whether you like me or not, I am certainly important.

If that I am trustworthy is not evidenced by the fact that I've been *entrusted* to run a business—and, for clarity's sake, it is neither my business, nor that of a close relative or friend; I truly did earn my place—then take, for example, my many other responsibilities, of which I'm assigned numerous simply because I am seen as most likely to perform them well. I'm always asked to bring the turkey at Christmas, because I always cook it to perfection. I'm the primary contact on three of my coworkers' medical forms. I am the one to call when there has been an accident. I don't think it gets much more trustworthy than that!

As for my place at the peak of society, that's a much more subjective matter. But, I would say that anyone who has several hospital wings in his name must have earned them somehow. I hear there's even a library somewhere or other that bears my name.

And then there's my desirability. For one who's unmarried, that might appear difficult to prove, but if the fact that I can name the bra size and preferred panty colour of every woman west of New York City sounds like an overstatement, then at least allow me to say as much for all the women in Buffalo!

The point, as I'm sure you've deduced by now, is that I am a person of great and significant needs, means, positions, and ideas. And as with all individuals of my standing, I'm unfortunately incapable of providing the exact same level of attention to every fine detail of my life. It is a regret of mine, to say the least, that I'm not perfect. But I should say that I'm close enough to suffice.

All of this is to say that it was particularly curious, this afternoon, when I became acutely aware of the sounds of the street. Of course, I walk the busy streets of Manhattan on a daily basis, and I know that there are sounds there, but I'd never particularly noticed the din before this afternoon as I was returning home from work.

Car horns blared loudly, shattering the feeble peace of my eardrums and aggravating a piercing headache. People screamed, spoke, whispered, swore. I even caught pieces of conversation— "…and that will solve everything…", "…*no sé nada…*", "…put it down! Gordon, *put it down!*"

Previously, there had been silence. That may not seem to make sense, but that's just the way things were. My ears had simply accepted no sounds until the streets forced them upon me.

If that wasn't and odd enough experience, I was further startled to discover a difference in the world about me. It was small, something I couldn't quite put my finger on, but the people, the colours, the shapes—everything was slightly off. Uncanny. All resembling what I know and have known for quite a long time—but none of it exactly *being* what I know.

I shook my head—which exacerbated my terrible headache, by the way—I was being silly. Perhaps the work had gotten to my head. Anyway, none of this was of consequence. I was unchanged and, if nothing else, I could rely upon that.

As I walked away from the busier streets, the sounds lessened to a hum. Finally, I had adjusted. The oddities of the other streets left me here, as well. Everything seemed much more *normal*.

As I reached my house, I examined the rustic, red-orange exterior, the brown oak door, the maroon eavestrough that separated my house from its connected neighbours. I looked to my upper window, at my petunias…but my petunias weren't there. They couldn't have fallen…or else…? I had to rush right upstairs to see to the poor flowers. I knew I shouldn't have planted them out of season!

Too concerned to put my shoes away, I threw them next to the rack without a second look. I was forced to pause my progress, however, at the floor-to-ceiling mirror near the front door. I was utterly disheveled! In fact, it was quite an embarrassment that I'd allowed myself to go to work in this white robe. My hair was a mess and a bit too long for my preferences. How had I let this happen?

Flattening the black mass—much greyer than I remember it being, but I must be getting to *that* age!—I shook my head in disgust before continuing at a much more reasonable pace through the kitchen.

Normally, I wouldn't have noticed, but maybe it was the cold sweat that had begun at the sight of my missing petunias, and had worsened at my image in the mirror, that made the intensive heat so apparent.

Looking for the source, I noticed with concern that the oven was on! I must have left it on this morning. Or else—what would I have made in the oven this morning? I couldn't even remember breakfast, but it couldn't have been that elaborate…

I was about to turn the oven off when footsteps approached. I froze. Someone was in my house!

I expected a long pause, a pregnant moment of terror and further sweating while I awaited the unwelcome intruder but, instead, the anticipation ended immediately.

A woman entered the kitchen with a start, grabbing her heart and opening her dry mouth as though I were a ghost. She was mid-thirties with long chestnut hair, green eyes, and blue toenails. I did not, however, know her bra size or panty colour. "Who are you?" she began in horror.

I puffed myself up importantly, as I'm wont to do in most of my business meetings, and even during a few business phone calls. Deepening my voice, I noted forcefully, "I think it is *I* who should be asking that of *you*. *I* live here!"

The woman stared at me with a combination of confusion and fear before she was interrupted by a high-pitched cry of, "Mommy, what's for dinner?" accompanied by a small and insignificant child traipsing into the room, stopping dead at the sight of me, and hiding behind its mother's leg.

"Go to your room for a moment," the woman instructed stably, and the child looked about to protest before a shot from those hard green eyes sent it racing away. To bring your child on a break-and-enter! The atrocity! The nerve!

Had she said "*your room*"?

The woman turned back to face me and said nothing for a moment. Then, "You're Wendell Burke?"

"In the flesh!" I said it indignantly to make my point, but I still raised a hand to my chest in pride as I spoke. "And you are...?"

She hesitated, "I'm the new owner..."

"You're..." I was ready to shut her down, but the shock of such a nonsensical statement struck me dumb.

Clearly, she recognized my confusion and jumped in before I could be left to blather uncertainly. "Your sister sold me the house almost ten years ago..."

"Ten years ago?! That's absurd..."

"You...you weren't supposed to..." she struggled before finishing in a small voice, "you weren't supposed to live..."

"Excuse me?" I was offended. How dare she?

"You're in a coma...*were* in a coma. Don't you remember?"

"I think I would remember if..." but then I remembered that I couldn't remember my breakfast, nor yesterday's, and I stopped.

"Your sister sold your house on your behalf. I live here now."

"No, no, *I* live here!" I insisted, but it didn't convince either of us. My piercing headache returned and my hands shot to my head. The woman took a step forward, as if to aid, but stopped suddenly, keeping her space. "What happened?" I breathed, needing some distraction from the pain.

"You were hit in the head. A pot of petunias fell on you…" I saw the empty window in my memory, and my eyes shot to the white robe. The hospital gown.

"I…I don't remember…"

"Maybe we should call your sister," the woman offered hesitantly. "And get you back to the hospital…"

"No!" I cried, racing for the door. Of my house. This was *my* house. I stopped, but I couldn't stay. I knew I couldn't stay. Flying through the door, I returned to the streets, the loud noises so unfamiliar, so distant, breaking through my skull until I felt like it would fracture.

This couldn't have been happening! Things like this don't happen to people like me!

The sounds got louder as I pressed onto the main streets. The honking of horns. The voices. The whooshing of the distant freeway. I ran until my legs couldn't carry me anymore, until the pain had spread from my head into my stomach and chest and I could no longer go on. On the stairs by a fountain, I collapsed and looked out at the city around me, so familiar, yet so different.

I scanned the world in search of self-confirmation, for the reassurance that none of this could be happening.

I found my negator in the form of a working man. His orange vest glinted in the late-afternoon sunlight; his torn jeans were stained with sweat. He was talking to a similarly-dressed man who leaned upon a truck, waiting to remove his materials and begin. Women wearing fashions I'd never seen before passed them by. Men wearing slogans that meant nothing to me weaved across my path.

And the man in the orange vest picked up his tools and started scraping the name off a storefront—a place I'd never been to before, although I'd walked this way every day for so long. An establishment I never would have dared to patronize. Not in this dirty part of the city.

Next to it was another store that I didn't recognize and, two down from it, another. I never noticed these kinds of things. I was too important to notice every detail.

But still, somehow, I could tell that the storefronts had changed.

He May Not Rise

"Happy anniversary, Bill," Dorothy raised her glass of sparkling wine high above the table to be sure that she wouldn't make contact with the candle at its centre.

"Happy anniversary," Bill returned with a semi-smile, although his shoulders twitched slightly as he said it, and he gripped his rum and Coke a little too tightly as he lifted it.

"To both of you!" came the most excited voice of the trio, as Kelly, Dorothy's mother, joined the excitement with her white wine, instigating the glass-clinking process. They all drank, Dorothy and Kelly taking in a sip while Bill chugged back the whole thing and looked around to flag a waiter for another.

If music was playing, it was too quiet to be heard over the din of conversation that permeated the restaurant—the tables a little too close together for complete privacy, but without compromising a degree of "niceness." The restaurant was far from a five-star locale, but it was meant to mirror one as best as possible for $25 per underfilled plate. Servers smiled like they cared but with judgement behind their eyes that challenged anyone who dared disturb their peaceful walkabouts.

"What's in the Bigoli Paste?" came the misguided voice of a curious first-timer a few tables over, and the mental sigh of the server was audible to all the regulars.

Ordering a rum and Coke was also sufficient for eliciting disdain, but Bill didn't much care. He enjoyed *Undici Sedie* for its food, not its ambience. Even then, it was more of a 'good-enough' establishment than a good one. Most importantly, it had seemed appropriate for the occasion. Low lighting for the romantic appeal, high prices for appearances—although his girlfriend was hardly going to be fooled into thinking that they were wealthy on account of one faux-glamourous outing. He probably could've picked somewhere better, if he'd known anything in the area, but they'd been here before and they knew what they were getting, which was always easier.

The food was delivered after precisely twenty minutes of waiting, and it was always this precise. Dorothy's lamb and green beans took up approximately half her dish, Kelly's charcuterie board held four slices of three different meats, two cheeses, and two slices of bread, and Bill's pasta formed a small spire in the centre of his plate.

"This is *so* good!" Kelly declared after three bites, nearly finished with her meal. "You know how I love my meat and cheese," she gave a knowing look to her daughter. "But this is really something else. I've never had anything like this before. I wonder what this meat's called," she identified the last long, thin, pink strip. "I'll ask the next time the waitress comes by…"

"It's prosciutto, mom," Dorothy offered.

"You can get it at basically any grocery store," Bill noted.

Kelly looked at him doubtfully for a second before shaking her head, "No, that doesn't sound right. I would've had it before. I'll ask when the waitress comes around, just to be sure."

And sure enough, the next time the server passed, Kelly flagged her down specifically for the sake of that question, while Bill looked away and disassociated from the inaudible sigh.

"So, it's called, *Prosciutto*," Kelly explained once the waitress had gone, pronouncing it with a mangled Italian accent, "Not…what did you call it?"

"Prosciutto," Bill cut in before Dorothy could answer. "It's the same thing."

"Well, maybe it's similar," Kelly suggested, and there was no point in continuing the conversation.

The dessert order followed, with Dorothy passing and Bill accepting that she would be eating half of his. Just as the server was preparing to walk away, Bill began, "And can I get…" but she was gone before he could make any more headway into his rum and Coke order.

Bill and Dorothy ate their respective halves of the tiramisu in quiet tranquility, enjoying each sweet bite and silently wondering—although they knew better—whether they should order another. Kelly, meanwhile, hummed every time her panna cotta touched her tongue, occasionally adding in a warm smile and a small shake of her shoulders for emphasis. "This was the best dessert I've ever had!" she declared, throwing one hand down upon the table as a mock gavel. Dorothy may have felt a twinge of disappointment at the dismissal of her cakes, but she didn't show it. "We need to come to places like this more often!"

"There's nothing stopping…" Bill stopped himself from being too blunt. "You can come back anytime. I can give you a ride…"

"No, I wouldn't want to come alone," she looked down, sadly, and that effectively concluded the discussion as neither of the other two knew precisely how to respond.

The drive home, which Bill made as quick as possible, rolling through stop signs and creeping on reds—habits that Dorothy disapproved of—was overrun by Kelly's backseat driving. Though Bill had learned to tune out the specifics long ago, knowing that she was still on about it was hardly pleasurable.

At home, while Dorothy and Kelly chatted in the kitchen, Bill immediately excused himself to the bathroom, where he washed his face and prepared for bed. Six years, they'd been together now. Six amazing years, and he loved Dorothy as much as ever. Tonight should have been one to celebrate that with passion and gusto but, as per usual, Dorothy would be uncomfortable with her mother in the next room, and that would put the kibosh on any extracurriculars.

When he heard footsteps on the stairs, it was time to vacate the facilities, and he returned to the bedroom to await his girlfriend's arrival. The sheets were thick and warm, and possibly too much for the summer, but Bill liked to have full control over his temperature, and the chance of it getting cold in the night was something he would not stand for. So, while Dorothy tended to sleep atop the comforter, Bill placed himself thoroughly beneath it, often pulling the padded cover up over his head for additional warmth.

"Did we really need to invite her to our anniversary dinner…?" Bill stage whispered as Dorothy entered the bedroom.

Shutting the door quickly, she shushed him, "Whisper!"

"Maybe, if I spoke louder, she'd get that we don't always want her there," he mumbled, deliberately masking the words.

"What was that?" and there was no doubt that she'd understood precisely. Dorothy stood with her hands on her hips, her dress almost seeming to tighten around her. Bill had a bad feeling that she'd be sleeping in pyjamas tonight.

There was no going back now, "I mean, do we really need to invite her to everything we do," he tried to sound reasonable without being pleading.

"It's just polite. Otherwise, we'd be leaving her here alone all the time," Dorothy was softening slightly, but she wasn't giving much ground. She pursed her lips.

"It'd just be nice if she'd *politely* realize that sometimes the invite's just a courtesy."

Dorothy looked to her boyfriend for a long time, statuesque, before she finally sighed and relented. "She's lonely. We're out all day. We finally come home and go out and leave her again? She just wants the company."

"Yes…" Bill conceded, looking away as he searched for the best way to keep from ending up single, "…but *every* time? I didn't even have to invite her today. I just said we were going to *Undici Sedie* for our anniversary and she said, 'That sounds fun, I'm looking forward to it' and got in the car."

"She's lonely," Dorothy reiterated.

"It's been…" he stopped himself. Dorothy's father had been dead for a year and a half now, and that was when Kelly had moved in with them, just two months after they had moved in together. The passing was unexpected, and it left Kelly without money or prospects. Putting her in a home would have been cruel, in Dorothy's estimation—at least, as long as she had her health and mind. The living situation had been meant to be temporary, but there had never been an exit strategy, and this was simply an unspoken understanding they all shared. "Maybe it's time we help her get a life outside of this house."

"She's never wanted to," it came with a shrug as Dorothy finally headed for the dresser. "She's not going to start now."

Bill wanted to protest, to push toward fighting for an alternative, but there was no good in it, so he settled upon, "Yeah, you're right."

With that, he rolled onto his side and pulled the covers up over his head—more to block out the light than for the heat. A few minutes later, Dorothy joined him, a few feet away, and both fell asleep.

*

It was still dark when Bill opened his eyes—he could tell although the covers shrouded his head. The stillness of the room betrayed the silence of night, which, in turn, amplified every miniscule squeak and twitch to ninety decibels. The bed creaked and Dorothy must have shifted in her sleep, turning to her side as she often did in the middle of the night. His eyes still only cracked to a squint, Bill took in the underside of the blanket slowly, still processing consciousness.

His right arm was asleep and nestled under his back, and the tingling discomfort was becoming present as he wakened. He shifted to extract the appendage…but he did not. As he made to pull his right shoulder up and to curl onto his left, no motion prevailed. At first confused, but imagining that he must have dreamt the failure, Bill attempted again. There was no doubt that he had tried this time, but still no movement. Mild panic set in and his breaths shortened. *Your arm's just asleep*, he told himself, *use the other one to move it.*

With all his effort, he tried to thrust his left arm upward and across his body—but, though this one was unpinned, it similarly would not move. Desperately, Bill kicked out with his legs, but they would not kick. No amount of strain would shift his static figure. As though his chest were being crushed, slowly but forcefully, he felt his breathing become shallower, each miniscule grasp at the air more difficult than the last. His eyes threatened to cry, but they could not move from their partial squint. If only Dorothy knew and could help him, shake him from his paralysis—but he couldn't call to her, much though he tried.

The fear of locked-in syndrome spread over him, followed by visions of being perceived as dead and buried alive, watching the coffin lid shake as an echoing rainfall of dirt pelted from overhead. Within, he wept and prayed for this to be a dream— but everything else was real and he knew that he was clinging to a desperate fantasy.

The quiet of night sunk in upon him until it was no longer quiet. There were footsteps in the dis- tance—slow, but deliberate, and approaching. Through the blanket, he could see nothing, and his breaths only became weaker as a result. Between the steps, low, indistinguishable whispers neared, their tone threatening. A few minutes later, a heavy banging in the distance began to punctuate each sentence, growing louder and louder, shaking Bill's eardrums and overtaking him with terror.

And just as it all increased and came to within inches of the covers, Bill found himself reawakening from sleep as though nothing had transpired. His eyes opened once more, this time to their full extent, and found the room as it was when he had awoken in falsity. His breathing was still rapid but beginning to take in the necessary air for survival, while the sweat that had burst out upon his forehead during the ordeal was as plentiful as if he'd bathed in it.

Once he'd panted his way through the first few desperate breaths and tested his fingers to be sure that he was removed from the terror, Bill began to relax, albeit sputteringly. His breaths now quiet enough to allow other sounds in, he recognized the still, calm comfort of silent night, only the standard cracks and creaks of a regular house to break the tranquility. Still wary, he removed the covers from his face slowly, peeking into the room around him while his eyes adjusted to the light. Tentatively, he made a sweep over the barren locale three times until he was sure that it was empty, aside from Dorothy, asleep beside him.

Removing his sweat-stained shirt and wiping his face with it before tossing it on the floor, Bill settled back onto his pillow and pulled up close to Dorothy, wrapping an arm over her bosom. He kept his eyes closed tightly and repeated to himself: *It was just a nightmare. It wasn't real.* And he prayed that, when he fell back to sleep, it would not occur again.

*

"It sounds like sleep paralysis," Kelly offered over the ham and eggs breakfast that Dorothy had prepared while Bill, still shaken from the previous night, had sat still with a hand upon his temple at the kitchen table. "I used to get it when I was a girl, but not much recently."

"No—no, I've never gotten it before. It wouldn't just start like that, would it?"

"Everything that starts just starts at some point," Kelly noted, although whether it was sage or meaningless was left for interpretation.

"Well, whatever it is, I just hope it doesn't happen again." He'd hoped to receive reassurance.

Instead, Kelly offered, "You really never know. Could be a one-off, could be the start of something. It could happen all the time or never, or just sometimes. I used to get it twice a week, like clockwork, and then it just stopped." She paused, "And then it started again. And stopped. And started again— and that was about forty years ago, now."

"I'm sure it won't happen again," Dorothy comforted in between mouthfuls of egg, but it was too little too late.

"I just want to know what I can do to stop it," Bill hazarded, almost hoping that Kelly would come up with a useful response.

Sure enough, she had something to add, "I tried almost everything. You just can't control it."

"Nothing even helped a little bit?"

"Nope!" she was much too cheery and Bill's fist tightened around his fork. "Just keep telling yourself it's not real and, eventually, it'll pass. I always found it was worse, though, when I had my blanket over my head."

Bill hummed, "Right, I'll keep that in mind."

"And try not to eat right before bed," Kelly added.

"I always eat before bed and this has never happened before, though."

"I know, it's just not good for you to eat so late." And Bill's hand clenched tighter. He felt tempted to have a late dinner tonight, just for the sake of it, but he pushed the thoughts away and instead asked Dorothy,

"How did you sleep?"

"Fine. Normal." She was surprised by the question and felt badly, as though she was gloating.

"That's good, that's good. Maybe we can watch a movie, tonight?"

"Yeah, that sounds good. It's been a while."

"I haven't seen a movie in ages!" Kelly chimed in, walking her plate to the sink and stopping in between Bill and Dorothy on the way by. "Nothing scary, though. I don't want to have a heart attack." With that, she cackled loudly while Bill shot Dorothy a look and Dorothy pretended not to see it.

Kelly had fallen asleep twenty minutes into the movie, but Dorothy nonetheless shot down Bill's suggestion of bringing the film upstairs to watch on a laptop in bed. She felt badly about it, just in case her mother woke up alone in the dark.

"She'll just assume it ended and go up to bed."

"What if she wakes up while we're taking the disc out of the player, though?"

"Then we'll tell her we didn't want to disturb her sleep, or that the movie's over."

"She'd know."

"So? We would've watched it in our room anyway, if, you know…" he gestured to Kelly.

"It doesn't matter. She's asleep now. We're missing the movie." She turned back to the screen and Bill was left with no option but to do the same thing, although he hardly enjoyed it.

Kelly awoke for the ending, asking "How long was I out? Catch me up," just as the final emotional moments were being played out and the credits began to roll.

"I'll watch it again with you another time, Mom," Dorothy offered, but Kelly waved it off.

"If I fell asleep that fast it can't've been that entertaining. Let's watch a comedy next time."

"This is starting to feel like one," Bill muttered, but neither heard him—although Dorothy knew it couldn't have been nice and gave him a shot in the arm.

"All right, I guess it's time for bed then. I'll see you both in the morning," Kelly retired to the stairs.

"We could watch another movie…?" Bill suggested, despite it being after 1:00am and knowing he had to work in the morning.

"Another time," Dorothy shook her head and led the way to bed.

Before heading upstairs, Bill chugged two glasses of water. Although he'd tried to put the previous night out of his head as best as he could, the threat of it still lingered, and the more impetus he felt to get up naturally in the middle of the night, the less likely he felt a repeat occurrence would plague him. If he hadn't felt bloated, he would have added another glass to the mix. He brought a full cup with him for the nightstand.

Dorothy was already in bed when he got upstairs, and Bill pressed himself close against her warm, bare body. Her state of undress was an apology, he recognized, but that was all. She was already attempting to sleep. Instinctively, he wanted to pull the covers over his head, but Kelly's warning from the morning discouraged it, and the additional cold disrupted his ability to rest for several minutes.

He hadn't even realized that he'd fallen asleep before he was waking again, his eyes half-open and his entire right side numb. *No*, he thought, but he knew. The moment that his fingertips refused to move, he was certain that no part of him would. *You're asleep*, he told himself, but he didn't feel asleep. Even a sleeping body could shift or turn. At least if he had been bound, he'd have been able to wriggle and squirm. This stasis was more like being drugged, totally frozen in everything but the whirring of his mind.

Dorothy was still before him, fast asleep and unaware. He wanted to prod her awake, to push his finger the few parts of an inch it would take to nudge the woman in hopes that she would wake, but he couldn't do even that. No matter what he thought, nothing would slow his breathing. The sweat returned to his forehead.

He shouldn't have slept with his back to the door. The footsteps were beginning again—slowly, but louder today, without the dampening of the cover overhead. The whispers were still incoherent but they also seemed less human in their increased clarity. The pounding returned, like a drum, preparing the troops for attack. The whispers turned to hisses as they neared, and shadows flickered across the walls, coming closer and closer.

It's not real. It's not real. It's not real! but he couldn't convince himself. Bill fought to rip his eyes open, to turn his head, to force any movement that might have helped him save himself. His finger was threatening to shake. If he could just get it to shift a little—anything at all. The creatures were almost upon him now and a dark figure flashed above his eye.

The muscle tensed and finally broke, moving slower than a starfish, but moving all the same, piece by piece, freezing every moment before he finally forced it to go, yet again. His entire body was covered in sweat now, and the figure that loomed in the corner of his left eye was leaning down, its breath starting to ruffle his hair. His finger finally made contact with Dorothy, but it was much too light to have an impact. He tried again, but the digit would hardly shift.

It's not real! Go back to sleep! he commanded, and while he couldn't feel his eyes closing, darkness overtook everything.

Just as they had the previous night, his eyes shot open as though nothing had happened and life returned to his limbs. Panting and gasping, Bill hugged himself tighter to Dorothy as his eyes scanned the room desperately. There was nothing here, and the only sound was Kelly's intermittent snoring from the other room. The temptation to wake Dorothy and ask her to hold him tightly was overpowered only by the disgust he felt at being perceived as a child, crying over a bad dream. But it was so much more than a bad dream.

The water that had not drained from his pores had settled in his bladder and, cautiously, Bill edged to the door, which he opened slowly, lest something be lurking on the other side. Nobody met his sight however and, quickly, he raced to the end of the hall, keeping his vision focussed solely on the end goal and never on what lay behind. The same trek brought him back to his bedroom and, now panting, he shut his eyes and concentrated on slowing his heartbeat until, finally, the incessant thudding lulled him to sleep, once more.

*

"It happened again," Kelly concluded upon walking into the kitchen in the morning and witnessing Bill, huddled under two sweaters, holding his coffee tightly, and staring blankly forward as though he'd just seen a ghost. "Hallucinations?"

He nodded once and hummed a yes. His voice was finally working again; he really should have used it, but he couldn't bring himself to at first. Finally, when he'd mustered up the strength, he asked, "How do I stop them?"

"You just get used to them. Sometimes, I'd pretend they were my friends, but that didn't work so well when they started yelling at me. Then, I'd just pretend they weren't there. It's all about pretending and making the most of these things we can't control."

Bill just shook his head. "No, there has to be something I can *do* about it."

Kelly shrugged, "There's nothing you can do—trust me, I'd know. Some things you just can't *do* anything about, and you just have to live with that."

But coming from the woman who was certain that there was a difference between prosciutto and *prosciutto*, Bill was far from convinced. The whole workday, he was distracted by thoughts of his nightly paralysis, wondering if he dared breach the

50

subject in front of coworkers, in search of reassurance. The thought of sharing his fears and weak-
ness with so many others, however, deterred him.
Instead, he spent the day being ineffective, hardly
listening to his colleagues and being chastised by
his managers. He was better than this.

The moment he got home, Bill walked past Kelly
with a curt hello and shut the door to his room.
Dorothy wouldn't be home for a few minutes at
least and, in the meantime, he would do as much research on sleep paralysis as he could—deliberately
doing so in the very place that had afflicted him. It
would not beat him down any longer.

Much to his dismay, he discovered that Kelly's
assessment was echoed by the majority of the online
community. Therapy might have been an option,
but, to Bill, that seemed like defeat. Improved sleep
hygiene came up a few times—but he'd never had
good sleep hygiene and he'd never had a problem
before. The inconsistency was what baffled him.
How could he defeat something with no identifiable
source?

The door clicked downstairs and he was out of
time. Dinner would come soon, and he had prom-
ised to play games tonight as a "family activity."
Most of the meal was spent in silence—Dorothy
had brought home takeout and Kelly was bent on
criticizing the greasiness while simultaneously com-
plimenting the flavour and bemoaning the combination for the entire meal. It suddenly struck Bill that,
for a woman who had spent her entire life cooking

and cleaning for her husband, she seemed surprisingly incapable of helping out around the house now that she was a guest.

Dorothy could read Bill's mentality with ease, but she was also well-aware that there was no comforting him when he got like this. Until a solution was found, he was best avoided and, where that wasn't possible, unprovoked. As such, it was with great care that she selected a game of rummy that she knew Bill was adept at winning. The distraction of success could sometimes draw him from his burgeoning anger. But Dorothy had misjudged the depth of Bill's obsession. It had such a powerful hold over him that a game he should have swept through with victorious aplomb ended in a pitiful loss. And another. And another. And while Kelly pressed for a fourth game—she was down two-to-one to Dorothy—her daughter could tell that it was more than just losing that had Bill shaking at the moment.

"How about something different?" she suggested.

"No, I want to play again," Bill offered coldly.

"Are you sure? Maybe…?"

"I think someone's ashamed to have lost to a pair of girls!" Kelly joked and, at the best of times, it would have been a misguided slight.

It took all that Bill had not to explode at the remark and, instead, he offered, "It's a good game. I'm enjoying it," through clenched teeth and shoulders.

"Well, good luck beating *us*!" Kelly declared, chuckling, while Dorothy hummed nervously and Bill dug his nails hard into his palm.

Three more losses were enough to end the evening, as Bill declared that he was "tired" at nine, and Dorothy agreed with the lie for all their sakes.

"I think I'll be up a bit longer," Kelly noted as the other two walked upstairs. "Just give me a holler if I make too much noise."

The whole way up the stairs, Bill muttered to himself, while Dorothy gave him ten paces of space. Finally, at the bedroom door, she asked quietly, "Do you want me to…?" she mimed going through the door. Bill glared for a moment before nodding once. Dorothy hated to see him like this and, the less she resisted, the more likely, she was sure, that he would recover.

When the door was finally closed, Bill took several deep breaths while leaning against the nightstand before admitting, "I want to go to sleep, but I don't." The strain in his voice was honest, and it hurt him to cede control to his privacy. But then, he knew that it had been obvious all along.

"It's okay," Dorothy put her hands on his shoulders and looked at him hard until he finally returned the stare. "I'll be right here. Nothing's going to happen. And if the hallucinations come back, just remember that they're not real. None of it's real. Anything can happen, but it doesn't matter."

With a breath, Bill relented, "I know, you're right. It's just…"

"It's hard. Don't think about it. The more you think about it, the more likely you are to make things happen. Okay?"

He sighed, "Okay." He took a breath, "I need to go get a glass of water…"

"I'll get it, just get in bed and relax."

Bill changed into his pyjamas and got under the covers. Under no circumstances should he have been tired this early, but the day had sapped his energy, and the bed felt comfortable in spite of its recent cruelties. The light was still on when he closed his eyes, but it clicked off a few minutes later, just before he heard the glass deposited on his nightstand. Shortly after Dorothy climbed under the covers, her cold feet on his legs and her arm wrapped around his neck, he fell asleep.

*

It was dark and he felt constrained, the pressure on his neck having grown over the course of the night. Bill's eyes shot open in the darkness and, before he could even think about his body, his breathing shortened. It was happening again. He didn't even try to move, to give his body the cruel possession that it so greedily licked away from him. Closing his eyes, he screamed within: *It's not real! It's not real! It's not real!*

The footsteps commenced outside the door, although there was no whispering or banging this time. It wasn't even affording him the courtesy of consistency. The sound of the door clicking open set his heart racing further. *It's your mind playing tricks on you!* The footsteps got closer. He could feel a presence behind him.

He didn't want to look—*It's not real!*—but he couldn't help it. He needed to know what was attacking his serenity. Throwing his eyes open once more, he espied the figure above, dark and shadowed, looking down upon him. He could make out no features, only that the being was standing, looming.

Bill's whole body started to shake with terror as he went cold, and he opened his mouth wide to gasp for air. It struck him, then, that he hadn't been able to open his mouth before. His fingers clenched upon demand. His legs bent at the knees. There was no paralysis, yet the thing was still here.

This time, he could do something about it. Wild and shot through with adrenaline, Bill cocked his legs and sprung up rapidly, the dark figure crying out and taking two steps backward before tripping and falling to the ground. Desperately seeking anything that would aid his reclaimed control, Bill's eyes settled upon the water glass, which he struck on the night table. Ignoring the tear as it cut his hands and the water that cascaded to the floor, he raised the remaining shards of glass and charged maniacally at the beast, which was slow to rise. Cries bellowed from around the room, taunting him, increasing his madness.

He was almost upon it when a second figure appeared from the shadows, diving across his path just as he thrust, and taking the brunt of the stabbing. It screeched out in pain and the initial beast cried out, as well. The light switch was just above their heads and Bill took the moment of shock to throw it on and destroy the creatures with light.

But as they came into view, Bill staggered back, confused. It was Kelly who sat upon the ground, crying out in despair, while Dorothy lay atop her, immobile, glass protruding from her chest.

Kelly. Kelly, who had come into the room to check on him in his sleep. That was all. She had come to check on him and, when he had attacked, Dorothy had accepted the blow.

Cold as the realization struck him, Bill fell upon the side of the bedframe and slunk to the ground. He was frozen by the horror before him, by the blood on the floor, by the lifelessness in the despairing Pietà. He shut his eyes. But, when he reopened them, the dream did not fade. He wanted to do something, to help, to erase it all from reality. But, as much as he tried to move his arms and legs, to sprout up and retake control of himself, he could not.

The paralysis would not allow it.

Storm Coming

Carl E. Masterham would have been a noticeable man where I'm from. But not in Mizerie. In Mizerie, he fits in with the average person. I haven't seen the average person, mind, but you can tell. He wears blue overalls over a grey-and-beige vertically striped shirt, stained with the grease and sweat of a man who spends his days in the fields and with his tractor, both on and beneath. His shoes are brown, scuffed, and shredded to fleeting wires in places, not too dissimilar from his hair, or what of it remains on his scaly scalp. The same can be said for his teeth, which scatter his piano-key mouth arbitrarily, two coincidentally adjacent ones sticking out from his bottom mid-right and over his upper lip when he shuts his mouth.

He looks alarmingly familiar, as though I've met him before. But that is impossible. I've never been to Mizerie in my life, and he's never left it. He has no car, no family, and wouldn't know a bus if he saw one. If his feet can't take him there, he isn't going, and there isn't very far that his feet could go, even if he weren't afflicted with a dramatic limp that lifts his left hip two feet in the air with every step.

It's been two weeks since I fell from the sky, a piloting accident on my first solo expedition. I think. The details are hazy. I recall the fire, and the jagged sheet of metal piercing my torso. I'm fairly certain there were screams of some kind, inarticulate and coarse, which I can only believe must have been mine.

That's about all I can remember, though. Even before that, everything seems like a blur, as though I dropped out of the sky and into a dream, one day, with no history. The only thing that gives me pause is the overwhelming sense of loss that has plagued the past two weeks, as though there's something hidden in the bleak distance of my memory, something left behind. Flickers of blurry dichromatic city life plague my brain at night, and sometimes during the day, as I think I'm focussed on the realities that are. I used to know these places, I'm sure, though I couldn't name one. But I do know how to live in them, and I likewise know that Mizerie is different.

Carl E. may be confident here, born, bred, and designed to traverse these empty meadows. But I'm not wired for them. When Carl E. pulled me out of my "sky tractor" and laid me on the cool, dewy grass, he'd stood over me for some time, clicking his tongue as he shook his head slowly back and forth, metronomically, keeping the rhythm of my heart as it threatened to die. I can still hear it sometimes, overlaid across those images of my nebulous past. "Click-clack, click-clack, click-clack." I almost feel as though my heart continues beating only because of his repetitive clacking.

"We'll get ya back on yer feet," Carl E. had reassured, dragging me up before the concussion preferred, and holding me upright as my fading body threatened to return to the ground. "Best get ya inside."

I'd longed for a bed and a warm cup of cocoa. Funny, I don't think I'd ever had a warm cup of cocoa before, now that I think about it. But my tongue knew what it would taste like before Carl E. had even put it on the rickety, unlacquered table before me. And without my ever having mentioned my desire to him, either. I ran my finger along the symbol etched into the table leg, an egg with a jagged edge at the top. Soft-boiled.

"Mmm, that's some good cocoa," I remember saying with an overdramatic flourish, letting the still-boiling liquid wash over my tongue, feeling nothing of heat after the fires that had engulfed me minutes earlier. Carl E. had smiled at that, a drunken guffaw, before limping with loud clops across the rotting floor to the kettle to pour himself one, as well. He didn't drink it, though. No, he'd let it sit and watched the sinuous streams of steam rise with intense focus and, the moment it had cooled to room temperature, he'd dumped it out the back window, "For the birds."

There are no birds in Mizerie.

Within a few days, I was back on my feet, surveying the lands with a cool and keen eye, suckling the beauty from the landscape to pacify my intermittently overactive brain. The rest of the time, it barely conceived of its surroundings.

Everything was meadow here. Even Carl E.'s shack seemed to disappear into nothingness after a few steps from its collapsing front porch, as though the entire structure had fallen to rubble and oblivion in the distance. And then there were trees. Somewhere in the distance, there were trees. Evergreens—tall, majestic, and bent in all directions. Behind them, there was more meadow.

I helped Carl E., as he required. "We cut the grass."

"For whom?" I wonder aloud. There is no one to see it but Carl E. and me, and nowhere to go on the other side.

"For the grass."

So, he rides his tractor and I accept his hand mower. The process is never done. It is continuous, as is the meadow.

And as we cut, we reseed, so that the meadow may continue.

In the hot, blazing sun, I ask Carl E., "How does it survive? The grass, I mean, in this heat, without water?"

Carl E. simply shrugs and wipes his nose on his sleeve. He hasn't changed outfits since the day I met him, and I realize now that neither have I. "There's a storm coming."

I look up to the clear, blue sky, not a cloud in sight. "How can you tell?"

But he's started toward the trees and I follow on instinct. As we approach, the heat increases inexplicably, until sweat mars my eyes and leaves me squeaking as I walk. "What is that?"

Carl E. sighs and leans upon his hoe—he's carrying a hoe, I discover. I hadn't seen the hoe until just now, and there's nothing to hoe anywhere around here.

"What…?" I begin, before I realize what he's staring at, shaking his head much as he'd done when he pulled me from the airplane. At the tip of one of those evergreen trees is a small stream of smoke, black and grey. The tip blows in the wind, although there is no wind. It's dangerously close to its neighbouring tree, which stands ominously still, like a candlestick just waiting to catch as the match manoeuvres its way to ignition. "We should do something," I press, examining Carl E.'s stagnant expression confusedly. This is, after all, his home that stands in danger of the inferno.

Isn't it?

Carl E. watches for a moment longer before looking straight up at the cloudless sky. Forlornly, he hangs his head. "We oughta be getting back," he warns, his voice caught in the in-between of melancholy and concern.

"But what about the fire?"

His eyes glare through me now, body tense and, for the first time, I see a new expression upon the man. It's not anger.

It's fear.

"I told ya, there's a storm coming."

He starts back toward the shack, or where I presume the shack must be in the invisible distance, laborious step upon laborious step that I still must run to catch up with. "My man, I believe you're deceived," I parry superiorly. "The sky is bluer than an asphyxiated face, today. Indeed, I haven't seen a cloud in a fortnight."

He makes no response, trudging forward forcefully, as though every step across the neatly mown grass is through quicksand. I watch his gritted teeth and reddening face for as long as I dare before finally facing forward.

And in a moment, we are surrounded. On every side, it presses in like an iron maiden, water falling in such thick streams that it's hard to believe that the world around us isn't a solid grey wall. We must have been instantaneously drenched, because I don't feel wet at all, and I don't see a drop upon my companion.

Carl E. stops, leaning upon his hoe, and looks out upon the storm. "We're too late," he muses casually.

"What now?"

"Now we wait."

"We'll be swept away in the deluge if it carries on like this! How long do these things tend to last?"

A wry smile creeps across the man's face, "Out in Mizerie, it doesn't rain much. But when it does, it makes up for it."

Somewhere behind me, the fire goes out.

Biting

Brendan didn't remember how he'd gotten to be face down in the snow but, as he awoke into the all-consuming night, he was more distracted by the cold solitude of his surroundings than with the specifics of his arrival. The road he stood upon, beneath the black of night, with a steady stream snowfall darting about his face, was lit by streetlights all the way down—it did feel as though 'all the way' meant eternally.

To the right, he saw nothing. To the left, nothing, still. It was the lights, against the dark, and his eyes still adjusting to the night, he told himself. That was what made him feel all alone, and this world seem so disconnected from the rest, as though a few steps in the wrong direction would send him cascading through time and space into a void of nothingness.

He pulled his grey, woolen trench coat tightly across his bones in a one-handed embrace as he spun against the wind, trying to get a good view of which direction to take, but both seemed wrong and, no matter which way he turned, the wind still pelted his face with icy white.

The way he'd first looked. That was good enough. It had to be. Neither stood out as expressly correct. Now, if he could only remember which way that was.

Brendan trudged along the road, toward wherever, not especially concerned about where it may take him, which surprised him, but he carried on. Something would be there, and that was more than was here.

It took him a few dozen yards before he realized that the snow melted on impact. Indeed, as if trapped in a poorly designed, early-2000s video game, the white stuff fluttered around and then, apparently, disappeared. The ground beneath him was clear, as though the city ploughs were guiding his way, an inch before him, but unseen in the dark.

Even his boots were wrong. Nothing stuck in the crevices, no hard-packed discomfort gathering beneath his soles.

But, again, as with all the other curiosities, Brendan found himself oddly unbothered. These things, which should not have been, simply were.

Subconsciously, the man chewed on the tip of his finger, a nervous habit of his years. He was wearing mittens—odd again. Brendan never wore mittens. He believed that to brave the cold was a sign of being a man. Though he would never go so far as to eschew the jacket.

The bitter taste of polyester increased as pieces of black material came loose in his mouth. He spat them away, but soon returned to biting.

The cold nipped at his nose, but Brendan felt no pain. He didn't even feel uncomfortable. A small part of him wondered if he would notice if he threw the garments away. But that numbness could have been a result of some injury, he considered, brain damage from the fall that had left him here, unaware of why.

A fall? No, that didn't seem right.

Hadn't he just been…?

No, he couldn't remember the last thing he'd done. Eating. He must have been eating, because he felt bloated and thick.

Eating alone on a Saturday night, as per usual, only his German Shepherd, Nibbles, to keep him company. He would share food off the table, act as though his girlfriend were stealing the last French fry.

And, naturally, Nibbles would turn his nose up at the human food. Sniff, judge, return to his food bowl, sniff, judge, go hungry until he could not wait to eat anymore. No, Nibbles only liked the unhealthy stuff, the pure fat-no nutrition kibble from the most popular brands. Brands that were more affordable than the healthy food Brendan insisted upon buying, even if Nibbles hated it.

He longed for that company now. Just the dog, forget anything else. Just to know he wasn't completely alone in the middle of nowhere.

And, as if called through the silence of the night, Brendan felt a brush against his ankle and turned down to see Nibbles following faithfully at his side, looking forward to the path, never up at his master.

Where was his leash? Brendan never walked him without a leash, for fear that he would run off and get hit by a car, one of the many that sped at

ungodly speeds, at all hours of the day, down his little side street in the city centre.

They should have been here now, breathing
down his neck and blowing him to the side of the
road. It was a wide street, clearly one meant to be
well-travelled. Yet, there was no one around but for
him and his dog.

He had trekked for an hour, maybe two. No
signs of civilization. But the streetlights carried on,
at consistent distances, suggesting that he was far
from the middle of nowhere. Never much of a
country boy, Brendan was aware of the country
enough to know that their locals knew the roads and
unwelcome visitors were left to be at the mercy of
headlamps and hope.

"Where are we, boy?" he reached down with the
partially chewed mitt to scratch behind Nibbles'
ears. The dog acted as though he did not notice as
he hop-stepped along his path.

A few more miles of finger chewing lay ahead.

Brendan was not tired, but he stopped.

He needed to think. Suddenly, he sought for that
anxiety that had driven so much of his life, had left
him walking a lonely road bereft of human contact,
working alone at home, never venturing into the
world around him.

That anxiety: it had kept him going, kept him
thinking. And, even if those thoughts were jum-
bled, at least they suggested movement, got him
somewhere.

He would never have gotten to his station in life
without that daily, raging fear pressing through him
and impelling action.

Now, he felt nothing.

So little nothing that he did not notice as his teeth
cut through the mitt and began picking at the finger
beneath.

Shaking his head after several minutes of una-
wareness, he attributed it to frostbite. His entire
body could have frozen during the God-knew-how-
many hours he'd been lying in the snow.

He pinched at the open hole above his finger, trying to seal it shut with pure will but, naturally, it
popped back open the moment he let go.

With a childish smile, he let the finger pop
through the hole, and wave to the elements.

But his smile was short-lived and the finger that
popped through was a clean, white, bloodless bone.

Where was that anxiety? Where was the stress?
He should have felt terror or sickness but, instead,
he stared, curiously, taking in the impossibility
without a single sensation. Even the desire to rip
off the mitten and examine his hand more closely,
to pray that it was a trick of the light, never came.

Slowly, he dragged down upon the mitt and let
more of the finger push through. A joint, another
bony phalange.

Brendan looked away, kept walking, resisting the
urge to keep biting at his finger. Nibbles took up
the trot the moment he started moving, as if he had
known that his master was about to walk.

"Good boy," he whispered. "Good Nibbles."

I haven't had anything to drink, but I'm not thirsty.

He glanced at a snowbank beside the road. Did he dare eat a little, quench the thirst that had hidden itself but that he knew must have been there? And what about Nibbles? Nibbles had to drink, as well.

He led the dog to the side of the road, or tried to. Nibbles would not follow. He stood in the centre of the street, looking straight ahead. Normally rife with separation anxiety, the German Shepherd seemed not to notice nor care that Brendan had left the main path. No matter, he would bring a clean, white patch of snow back for the dog, and he would be happy for it. Nibbles loved licking ice almost as much as he loved licking Brendan's hand.

Brendan searched for clean snow and found that all of it appeared clean. Not a speck of dirt, a single pebble, besmirched the clear white mounds before him. He cupped a wide handful and brought it to his face. Opened his mouth with a clatter. And felt the unmelting cold fall from the sides of his face.

Instinctively, he felt up for his cheeks and noticed nothing through the mitts. He whipped his hands about until the garments fell away and tried not to look at the sharp, bony hands that he extracted from them. He felt his cheeks, drawing his fingers along his maxillae. And through the holes where mandible met zygomatic arches. There should have been flesh there, muscle.

He found empty space. His bones drummed against his bones, click-clacking in the silent night air. But he did not panic, could not panic.

He returned slowly to his pet, who seemed to take no notice of his deathly figure. Nibbles was normal. He had not been stripped bare, cut away in the night. He ran his hand through the dog's hair. "Everything's fine, right, Nibbles?"

He slid his carpals under the dog's chin and lifted it to face him.

The normally dark and loving eyes were cold and empty. The dog was there. Yet, he was not inside.

But Brendan's eyes were drawn more to the creature's lips, where a dangling string of pink and red hung lifelessly in the cold. "What did you eat, boy?" Brendan asked perfunctorily, but he knew.

Carefully prying the mouth open, he plucked the pieces of human flesh from between the teeth. His flesh. Watched it fall to the ground, piece after piece, seeming to grow inside the dog's mouth until a human's worth of meat lay upon the ploughed, snowy road.

The poor animal had poisoned itself on whatever had poisoned him.

Brendan sat, emotionless, though he wanted to feel emotion, gently stroking the head of the dog, instinctively, while Nibbles, of its own instinct, licked at his bones, nipped at his fingers.

They held this position for a while, until Brendan grew weary of the repetition and lay prone upon the asphalt.

He felt nothing as the dog crunched upon his leg, his arm, his skull. And, slowly, the shattered fragments of his bone were captured by the whirling chill of the wind and floated away into the death of the night. Just fragments of white, blown away in the biting storm.

The Red Fox

My earliest memory is of the Red Fox.

I was fairly young, young enough that I shouldn't remember anything, but that fox always stood out. That and the colour of everything. All red, even redder than the fox, itself. Pulsing lights against the formerly white walls, pulsing in pace with the dark, electronic hum of the music.

I wasn't supposed to leave my room. I don't remember this part directly; it comes from my next memory—a memory of the following morning, when I was in bed, my bedroom door locked from the outside, and all I could hear was my parents yelling, fighting. I heard a slap. A car door slam.

"I told him not to leave his room!" my father had shouted.

My mother had said something about chopping his balls off. At the time, I thought she'd meant he wouldn't be allowed to play sports, anymore, and I thought that funny, since my father was fat and lazy and never played sports. At least, not any that I understood.

After that, I didn't see my father anymore. Every year, on my birthday and at Christmas, my mother would rush to the mailbox, find the letter he'd sent, and burn it in the fireplace. Every year, I would ask why. Every year, she would tell me that there are things no boy—no *person*—should ever have to know.

I never dared to ask her about the fox, even as it haunted my dreams through childhood and into my early-twenties.

When I woke up drenched in sweat and piss, I would change the sheets before she could find out. Of course, she knew. It wasn't as though I knew how to do the laundry at five years old.

To this day, I don't know why I didn't ask. It would have been the natural thing for a child to do, but I suppose I wasn't a natural child.

Natural children don't enjoy the darkness of the garage, but that's where I spent my days, when my mother wasn't home to tell me not to. Just sitting there and feeling the energies. Something had happened there, I could sense, but I didn't know what. And it was a part of me.

In my dreams, the Red Fox would come, larger than a man, and just stare at me through plastic eyes. He would never approach, never speak. A quiet standoff of two friends who were adversaries by existence and not by ill-will.

As I got older, the dream became sharper though the memory became duller. If not for my father's perpetual shunning, I might have thought I'd imagined the whole thing.

But every time I stood in the hall, a few feet outside my bedroom door, I could feel the physical, visceral memory coursing through me. And that's how I knew it was undeniably real.

I left home when I was eighteen. I didn't have money or a place to go, but I couldn't be around my mother any longer. She had darkened on that day thirteen years earlier and had never found the sun again. I always assumed it was the loss of my father that had done it to her, but it wasn't. It was that she'd ever had him at all.

On the first day of university, Carlo invited me back to his home. He was an apathetic senior with no goals and a lifetime supply of marijuana. I wouldn't smoke, but I didn't mind him smoking, and the second-hand poison finally shut my mind off from the realities that had haunted my brain for so long.

I never forgot them. But they weren't *there*, anymore.

I found a job as a butcher's assistant to work my way through university and to pay half the rent. Not that Carlo was ever aware when I was a few days late. His brain was so fogged over by the time he was twenty-three that I could have told him that I was his father and he would have believed me. I did, once, when I wanted him to clear out for a few days so I could have some alone time with Lynsy. By the end of October, Lynsy was well worn and off to find a new fit, and I thought I'd never see Carlo again. But then, there he was one morning, in the refrigerator, asking whether we had any eggs and drinking scotch like time was meaningless.

I suppose he was right about that.

Daily, I would come home, stinking of raw meat, covered in blood. I wore the apron because I had to, but I didn't mind getting the mince on my clothes.

If Mr. Guilio hadn't been watching, I might have snuck a bite, just to know what raw hamburger tasted like. But I didn't dare, and the motivation left me as soon as I was away from the shoppe.

I got fired when I was twenty-five and he found me facedown on a rack of lamb. He thought I was drunk but I hadn't touched alcohol in my life. What I was was lost, fading in the sense of time and wondering at the point of everything, knowing there was something out there, calling to me, but never knowing what it was.

I stole the rack of lamb on the way out but cooked it. My teeth had paused inches from the raw meat, unable to finish the task.

To pass the time and pay the rent, I took a job at a meat packing plant. Mr. Guilio wouldn't give me a reference but, apparently, the standards weren't high. I never got to touch the meat there, but I could smell it and the animal sense within me wanted to taste it, once again.

Gavin understood.

I never told Gavin the ways in which my mind worked—I never told anyone. But he could see it in my eyes, the way my nostrils flared as a fresh batch came in, the way I'd lift my mask to "scratch," but really to get a better sense of the gorgeous aromas.

He whispered in my ear, one night shift, "It's the wrong meat." And we both knew exactly what he meant. In the lunchroom, he'd pause over the raw hamburger he brought with him every day but he'd never take a bite. I couldn't bring myself to go that far, to torture myself like that, but we both could feel the sensation.

We never spent time together outside of work, nor did we spend time with our other coworkers. They could never understand and we could never admit to what we knew, what we could feel.

I've always assumed that it was Gavin who left the paper under the front door. Carlo found it and threw it away, but I noticed it sitting on top of the can. Carlo always forgot to lift the lid in his forays into different planes of existence. Usually, the lid was topped with banana peels, mould, rotten lefto-vers.

The paper card had only an address and a time. No name. But it was for me.

The pulsing music made its way through my feet, into my soles, and up through my body, even from half a mile down the street. Nobody else could feel it.

The house looked no different from any subur-ban monstrosity. Bleak and red-bricked; cold. But heat emanated from within and sucked at the body like a moth to a flame. A fox to a carcass.

Within, the electronic music pulsed at volumes so low that no one could hear them, but everyone could feel them. Everything was a sensation and nothing a reality.

The walls were basked in red lights, dim yet blinding, as though the entire world was staring at the sun through closed eyelids.

On a table in the centre of the room sat strips of raw meat that looked cured but weren't. The smell gave it away.

A smell that mingled with sweat and the deep, musky aroma of lust, sex. Not the sex of love, but that of realization, of release in a manner that no other person could understand.

As I paced into the centre of the room, the bodies emerged around me, milling about as though their minds were shut off and instinct alone guided their feet. I scanned the room for Gavin, for a face that I knew, and found that I knew them all.

Animals. The faces of lions and bears, wolves and hyenas. The visages beneath melded with the ones on top. I, alone, was human.

And, there he was, in the corner of the room. The only one immobile and staring at me as he had done so long ago.

The Red Fox.

My father.

I was not supposed to approach him, nor acknowledge his existence. None of us were here, we all understood. So, I turned away and followed the edges of the room, the dark corners, the exits that would not take me.

At the staircase, I descended, hand running against the smooth, white wall as I went. It was darker here, but light no longer mattered.

The basement was empty, cold, barren. It reminded me of the garage and I felt safe. And the smell—it was the same, exuding the identical sensation to the one that had drawn me for years.

I walked the edges of the room, tasting the old, familiar feeling, before finally turning my gaze to the centre of the basement.

There, tied by the wrists and ankles to hooks that jutted from the ceiling and floor, was a man. He wore no mask. He wore nothing at all. His back was bloodied, as if from a whip. His face was weak, tired, desperate.

A small lurch attacked my stomach, but it was not one of disgust or terror. It was

excitement.

Unconsciously, I took a step toward the bound, naked man, then another. I don't know how long I stared at the helpless figure before I realized the sensation of bodies around me. I did not need to look to know it was my father at my shoulder, the others now circled about the room.

The whip was inserted into one hand. The cudgel into the other.

A voice whispered in my ear and it was the voice of my father but, equally, the collective voice of every body in this room. Of Gavin. Of the unspoken truth. Of the Red Fox.

"Take him. He volunteered."

My first strike was light, weak.

Tension rose within the room. Had they made a mistake? Did I truly belong?

The next one was easier, and the next easier still.

The thought of my father and what he was doing on that night in my childhood…

It drove me.

He was not the Red Fox, then. But that was the night he became the Red Fox.

My fury grew, my disgust, my hatred.

And so, too, did my lust at the smell of the meat, cooked only by the kinetic energy of lashes, falling, otherwise raw, to the floor about the man.

But I was not angry at my father for what he did and what he is. I was furious at my mother for what she knew, for what she had allowed. She had known and had always known, yet had said nothing. Not until it was almost found out.

That was the sickness that I could not abide.

My mind reduced to nothing but the rhythmic beating of whips and cudgels, blood and flesh. I could feel the pieces of human upon me and taste them on my lips. The right meat, finally in its place.

And, when I had finished, covered in sweat and piss, I collapsed upon the floor and felt the pulsations carry me away.

*

I awoke in the shower, naked and dry, reality a blur and everything unfamiliar. The red lights were gone and sound had returned to emptiness.

Staggering, my shoulders tense, I forced my way out of the room and down the stairs. There was no

one home. I didn't need to search the house to feel
that the presences were gone, one and all.

Perhaps, it had never happened.

There was no blood in the basement, no meat on
the table. Everything was clean and fresh. Lifeless
in its insistence upon being alive.

I found clothing in the upstairs bedroom. A single pair of pants, a single shirt, a single pair of
socks, a single pair of shoes. All fit perfectly, but
they were not mine.

They *were* not mine.

I was about to leave when, hand upon the front
door, my eyes were arrested by the only thing in this
entire house that was out of place, sticking out from
behind the sofa. I could see only the tip, but I knew
what it was.

Holding it lightly between my fingertips, as
though it might break, I cautiously lifted the mask
to my face and fastened it in place.

My feet carried me to the couch and sat me there,
waiting, ready for the next time, prepared for the return.

It had always been mine but only now was it me.

After all those years.

I was the Red Fox.

Why Couldn't It Have Been Yesterday?

When Karen awoke, some sick part of her knew that Horatio was dead. Not that she cared. Not really. Even if he *had* been just a child. It was all some perverse part of the inevitability, and the energy—Horatio's cold, dying energy—that filled her bedroom was a serene reminder that the rest of time would be, if just, easier.

She pulled on a baggy ripped shirt—not hers, but it was now. She'd slept in her holey jeans.

When she walked into the kitchen, slightly run-down but not dirty—never dirty, she'd cleaned it yesterday; she couldn't help it if she had to clean with rusty water—Brandon was already at the cheap wooden table, the one Morgan had propped up on dusty copies of the Bible, Quran, and a few other religious books that none of them had any interest in reading, before dropping dead of God-knows-what, possibly lightning strikes from a variety of disgruntled deities.

A bottle of half-finished gin sat open on the table and Brandon was throwing back what looked like his third or fourth shot. Two glasses brimming with the repugnant liquid sat at the other end of the table.

"Horatio?" Karen asked dumbly. Brandon's bloodshot eyes, as he looked at her like she was

stupid, confirmed the story. He looked down at the
shot glasses and back up at her.

"I'll pass. Damn it, Brandon, it's not even nine
a.m."

At that, Brandon snorted. "You're keeping
track?" Not drunk yet. His voice wasn't slurred,
which was always his tell. Probably hadn't been at
it for that long. Or maybe the tolerance was finally
just getting up there. Crazy to think he'd been hesi-
tant to try a sip of beer when they'd first arrived.

Karen moved to the fridge and extracted a small
container of overcooked, fatty meat. "Half and
half?"

Brandon blew air through his lips and looked
away. "We got more now. I'll eat later."

"Guess that's one way to look at it," Karen
hummed, disapprovingly.

"You gonna do it or should I?"

"What, cook you lunch?" she gave a single, sar-
castic 'ha'. "You're on your own, buddy."

"'Til you get hungry later."

"Hey," she pointed a rusty fork at him, "don't go
Little Red Henning me. I took my turn."

"And so did I!" he growled, the blood in his eyes
gleaming red, shoulders tense and neck bulging.
But, a moment later, he'd looked away, shaking his
head. "I know, I know. We all did. We all did it
except Larry, God bless the bastard."

Brandon twirled his shot glass in his fingers, letting a little gin spill onto his fingertips before slam-
ming the thing down. His dark black hair was

matted against his head from the heat of the day and it would only get worse as the sun rose and the alcohol kicked in. In that moment, she almost pitied him. Not completely. Not when they'd all been there—he didn't get to be special. But she'd never given him credit for his youth before. Twenty-five, maybe six now, for all they knew.

At twenty-nine, she wasn't much older, but it *felt* older, somehow. Felt like she should've been the one in charge. But most of them had been older than that. Carl was forty. Mohammad sixty-two. Jean had to have been ninety, if not a clean hundred, and she'd still managed to outlive most of them. It had been so easy to fall in line, to take leadership from someone else, that Karen had forgotten her own strength.

"Look," she reasoned, "I'll cook if you do the prep."

"Naw, forget it," Brandon slammed his hands down on the table, its legs creaking, threatening to break under his weight. "Probably my turn anyway."

He left the room, three untouched glasses still on the table. "Brandon," she called after him, half-heartedly, but he probably hadn't heard her. Even in this little, rotted shack, the walls seemed thick, especially so when you whispered a name you ought to have screamed.

Rogan had found that out the hard way, when they got him.

Never stand close to the window—open or closed—that was the rule. He *knew* that was the rule.

"Jean." He'd cried out for Jean in the hoarsest of whispers as the fingers tightened around his neck and drew him into the bush. Dead. Gone. A waste to them all.

And, half-blind and knitting, she hadn't heard him until he was already being dragged along the broken shards of glass, leaving a trail of red along the garden path as a few globules of blood cascaded down the sill and to the floor.

It was two hours before Jean passed along the news to the rest. After all, there wasn't much they could do.

*

Forty minutes passed of forks and knives scraping on wood, like a broken pencil across a chalkboard— the plates had been sacrificed as weapons long ago—before Karen broke the silence. "Thanks…for dinner."

Brandon glared at her. "What's the rule?"

She clenched her jaw. "I know, I know." *Never acknowledge it. NEVER acknowledge it.*

Karen toyed with a sinewy piece of meat before reconsidering and putting it down. Might as well save it until tomorrow. Hard to know how many days they'd have to wait. Or if it even mattered.

She threw her leftovers in the fridge with the rest. Brandon didn't look up as she left for the bedroom.

She could reread another book. Plot another futile map. It just all seemed so pointless. Conversation was out of the question. That had gone with Morgan—must've been, three weeks ago? Or maybe two.

Or one.

At least Horatio had provided bad conversation, which she now realized was better than none at all.

A crash came from the living room, something like a violent crack. Not glass, but—the thin wooden boards they'd used to cover the hole where Rogan had been taken. Snatching up the broken beer bottle that she'd kept in the corner of the room she'd once shared with Jean, she rushed out into the hall, nearly colliding with Brandon, suddenly wakened at the sound and panting hard.

"What was that?"

"What do you think?" he shot back, annoyed. Together, they turned into the living room and confirmed their fear.

The entire wooden board was cracked into pieces, shattered like glass on the living room floor.

"They're inside," Karen breathed, hand tightening around the bottle.

Brandon approached the hole, "It was only a matter of time…"

"Don't get close!"

"Let them pull me out," he snapped. "If they're in here, I might as well be out there."

Karen said nothing, inched into the centre of the room, which felt, somehow, safer.

"Looks like it was shot through," he analyzed.

Feeling safer with company than alone, even if it meant approaching the danger zone, Karen edged closer to examine the viciously shattered hole. "With what, though."

"Whatever it is," Brandon glanced up, meeting her eyes—not confident, not afraid. Just rational— he gestured to her bottle, "that thing ain't gonna do much against it."

In unison, they backed away from the window, searching around the room with their eyes. There were only so many places they could be. It wasn't that large of a house.

"They could be anywhere."

"They could be everywhere."

"Do we make a break for it?" but the moment she said it, a figure appeared beyond the window, in the distance, just along the treeline. It was dark and he was in black. But it was no coincidence. He was waiting.

"If it's just him…" Brandon bit his lip as a second darkly clad and hooded figure presented beyond the glass of the room's second window.

"We'll have to fight them off eventually," Karen reasoned.

But Brandon shook his head. "On our terms, not theirs. We have no idea what's out there, how many of them there are."

"We don't know how many are in *here*, either."

"We know we can't just run for it. We *saw* what happened when Billy tried to run for it. We pick them off. One by one."

Teeth clenched, but knowing, somehow, that he was right, Karen grunted, a deep, scratchy grunt. "Why?" she breathed. "Why, why, why, why, *why*? Why did it have to be today? Why couldn't it have been..."

Brandon scoffed, "What? Tomorrow? The next day? Christmas 2052? They were waiting to come, for us to be weak, so they could pick us off and end it. What does it matter when they did it? It was going to happen eventually."

Karen swallowed hard, bit back her rage, "I was going to say, 'why couldn't it have been yesterday?' Why couldn't we have just gotten the damn thing over with, already?"

Brandon paused. "Because then it wouldn't have been this easy."

A hooded figure appeared at the entrance, the exit. A third emerged from a closet and a fourth climbed—practically glided—through the window.

"Listen, Brandon," Karen began, mouth dry. "If this is the end, I want you to know. I never much cared for you. But I'm still gonna do my best to keep you alive."

Brandon nodded slowly, eying up their assailants. "Same here, Karen. Same…here…" With a quick flash, he leapt for the table lamp that glowed orange from the side of the room and yanked it from the wall, wielding it above his head with a battle cry. As the plug came detached, they were plunged into darkness, the nearly-new moon their only vague sense of vision.

Karen rolled across the couch and struck her bottle at where the figure had blocked the entrance, missing flesh but catching garment. She felt the wind from the blow coming for her head and ducked. Something struck the wall and she oriented herself within the room from the sound.

Behind her, voices cried out; someone was hit, badly.

She broke for the door, wishing she'd turned on the hall light on the way down. But she'd been in such a rush. A slice crossed her Achilles, tearing skin, but not quite deep enough to do real damage.

She fell to the floor on impact, spinning around wildly with her bottle and, unexpectedly, making firm contact that resulted in a cry. A man's voice.

The triumph was short-lived, however, as the remainder of the bottle shattered in her hand, leaving her with a nub of a neck and deep cuts across her fingers. Leaping up, she ran along the darkened hall, willing her footsteps into silence, but grateful for the sounds of those that followed. She knew she had a big lead. If she could just get to safer territory…

And then she was falling, sailing through the door to the basement, elbow smashing across the banister, knee against the wall. Face against…

…somehow, her hand saved her head from the cold, dirt floor, though it did nothing for her wrist, which turned badly upon impact. She cried out, wishing to conceal herself but knowing they knew where she was.

Between adrenaline and fear she managed to push herself to her feet, the pain in her wrist so blinding that she was sure she was going to pass out. Couldn't stand. She stumbled back, crashing against the cold, concrete wall. Falling in a clatter atop a pile of her friends' and acquaintances' bones.

Slowly, the footsteps crept down the stairs. Tap-Tap-Tap, Thud-Thud, as they hit the dirt floor. A crack—the figure stretching his neck in the dark.

A breath.

"Why are you doing this?"

Thud. Thud.

There was no time to wait for answers. She grabbed the nearest thing to her good hand and fired it at him. Jean's severed head.

She heard it connect in the dark and the figure stumble back.

For a stunned moment, the intruder registered the reality of the weapon before charging, seeking to end his mission immediately.

And Karen began throwing body part after body part, head after femur after ilium, the more recent of them still slippery with rancid matter.

He backed away, charged again, backed off once
more.

Karen reached down for more, anything that
would lift.

Her hand spiked against a broken tibia but she
barely felt the pain with her other wrist still throb-
bing. She snatched up the thick bone and struggled
to her feet.

Thud. Thud. Thud, thud, thud.

And just as the figure came near enough that she
could feel the aura of his body heat, Karen thrust the
tibia forward and felt it pierce the soft skin of the
stomach, angled upward to the heart.

Her assailant fell back and she landed atop him,
driving the weapon in deeper and deeper.

"You. Won't. Escape. It. Never. Ends." he
sputtered as blood pooled in his mouth. And then,
he died.

Karen tugged and turned until she had finally
dislodged the weapon before rising. She felt around
with her foot before she found his neck and pressed
down for thirty seconds, a minute, five minutes.
Just to make sure he was dead.

No breath. No pulse.

She breathed a sigh of relief. Satisfied, she crept
back to the stairs. Others would be coming soon.
She waited there for them, squinting up into the
barely moonlit hall, eyes still not fully adjusted to
the dark.

But no one came. For an hour, no one came.

Fear surging through her, but knowing there was no other way, she slowly crept up the stairs. Near the top, she listened, but heard nothing.

At the top, she stopped, bone at the ready. No one charged at her. Nothing moved.

Feeling along the wall with her injured arm, she managed to find the light switch. The pain in her wrist as she turned it on nearly sent her to the ground again, but she threw a shoulder into the wall, willing herself to stay upright.

Someone should have attacked. She was an easy target.

But nothing.

She dragged herself along the empty hall, glancing into rooms along the way and finding them bare.

The living room was ahead and, with it, the end. She knew that without knowing it, just as she had known that Horatio hadn't made it through the night.

The room was still in darkness, and there was no light left to illuminate it, but the soft gleam from the sliver of moon and the hall were sufficient.

Brandon lay in the centre of the room, eyes open, as was his chest. He was rigid. Had it been more than an hour she'd waited?

Beside him lay an equally mangled man, face shrouded, but wounds exposed to the world. Another lay a few feet away, on his face, but unlikely to rise again, considering the fire poker through his back.

There was one more—where was he? She slipped into the room just in time to hear a moan from the window. The lamp lay, cracked, to his side and his eyes had rolled back in his head, but his hood had come off and he lay before her, just a man. Just a dying man.

She put a shoe to his neck, as she'd done her previous kill. "Why?" she glowered down at him. "What's the point of it all?'

For a moment, he stopped moaning, tried to focus his bleary eyes upon her. He swallowed, his pale white face covered in bloody blonde hair. He licked his lips, but there wasn't water left in his body, let alone his mouth, to provide comfort. "I could ask you the same question."

Karen hesitated. "No." Her shoulders tensed, shook slightly. She removed her foot and bent down close to the dying boy. Maybe fifteen, eighteen years old. "You can't." She drove the broken tibia into his heart and watched the life flow away from his worthless face.

Barely thinking about her actions, she approached the fireplace and removed two pieces of wood, which she absently hammered over the hole in the window. It wouldn't keep them out, not if they really wanted to get in. But nothing would. And they'd come again.

But it was the symbolism of the matter that struck her, the semblance of safety. And the reminder to keep out. They wouldn't bother her again for a while. She could feel it.

She could live with the bloodstains in the carpets and drapes—she'd seen worse, she'd lived with it all. But the smell was too much.

She spent the following day carefully dragging the bodies into the basement, where she could work in peace—a process delayed by the pain that still shot through her arm. But there was no rush and nothing better to do.

She stripped the clothes from the bodies and scrubbed them as clean as she could.

She started with Brandon, partially out of respect and partially so she wouldn't have to look at him, looking at her, any longer. By this point, the process was second nature. She stripped the skin and the flesh, cleaned everything she could off the bones and into a bucket. She salvaged the organs that hadn't been destroyed in the previous night's battle, but she left the skulls intact. Never the brains— she'd heard that somewhere.

In some ways, it was fortunate that Horatio was the only one to die recently. The freezer was empty and none would go to waste. She still had a few days of Horatio remaining. No point in wasting anything until that was gone.

Sweating and tired, she didn't even think about eating until night had fallen. Too fatigued even to bother warming it up, she carried a calf into the

living room and gnawed upon it thoughtfully, gaz-
ing out into the night.

"I could ask you the same question."

Pathetic.

She couldn't see them, but she knew they were
there. Watching her. Waiting.

"What's the point?" she asked them, but differ-
ently, this time. She didn't want their master plan—
she sought their motivation, their hope. "You'll
never understand."

She took another bite and spat a bit of fat upon
the ground where the dead boy had lain.

"No," she shook her head. "You'll never understand."

The Fifth Passenger

Melanie

There's a pop song playing on the radio about a girl who would die for her man and Adam is mouthing the words as he drives. He must think he's being covert, hiding the fact that he's into what's pretty obviously a "girl song", but he can't help letting a few sounds escape as he gets into the chorus. I'm tempted to needle him a little but, thankfully, I don't have to, as Jack pipes up from the back seat,

"What's his name, Adam?"

Blushing, although it's a little hard to notice it on this dark, unlit road, our driver tenses and squeaks out a "What are you talking about?"

"The guy," Jack prods. "The one you're singing about."

"What? It's a good song," Adam mutters sheepishly.

"It's really not, though," Danny chimes in from his spot behind the driver's seat.

"Yo, it's got a good hook, that's all," Adam speaks calmly and raises his hands in a nonchalant but defensive manner. Then, with a quick jolt, he throws his fingers back onto the wheel as a surprise curve in the road nearly sends us off it.

"Nice one, there," Jack comments.

"Do you want to drive?" Embarrassment has rendered his tone dry.

"How about no." I can hear Jack slide down lower in his seat, relaxing for the remainder of the journey.

Jack probably would know this route better than any of us, and considering the less-than-ideal driving conditions this late at night, it might be best to put the wheel into his hands, but it's Adam's car, and besides, Jack did his part to contribute to this trip already. It was his idea to invite the three of us down to hang with his family in Chicago, and while it was admittedly probably not a purely altruistic offer, it was still a generous one—especially considering the way his Aunt and Uncle had spoiled us over our week there.

This was originally meant to be a family reunion that Jack was trying to stick to the outskirts of by having us as buffers, but when a cousin's dog got sick and a grandmother pulled out to avoid the journey, it all ended up crashing down. By then, Adam, Danny, and I were committed, though, and Chuck and Diane were ready to welcome us.

I still feel like we should have done more than just make them dinner on the last night—especially when they insisted on buying the groceries—but I don't really know what else we could've done. They just kept offering us food and alcohol, and occasionally a ride into the downtown core. It was too much to politely decline all of it. All the generosity did kind of throw off the plans I'd made, but never for the worse. I'd spent a lot of time mapping out the city—which I'd only been to once before, and briefly—finding routes and money-efficient means of getting around. That kind of thing always fell to me. I had the day plans ready, the bookings lined up. They could probably manage it themselves if they had to, but I like to get everything ready—planning and preparing for the future are basically the only things that keep me sane. And I definitely don't like owing anyone money—so I'm happy enough to take on the responsibility most of the time. I probably could have saved a few hours if I'd known just how spoiled we were going to be, but I can't complain.

"I need a drink," Jack groans from the backseat. It's been a long drive already and we still have an hour or two to the border, not to mention a pretty decent trip on the other side of it. At twenty-one, he's the youngest of the four of us by two or three years, and his drunken party-loving disposition is keeping us all in our early twenties even time is pushing us out of them.

"We can stop for a drink once we're in Canada," I suggest.

"It's going to be, like, one in the morning, though!" the frustration is unnecessary.

"I'm just saying we could."

"Wow, thanks guys," Adam comments lowly, "all planning on having a party without me, then."

"True," I'd forgotten that little bit about the driving.

"Nah, I definitely think we should stop," Danny needles.

"If you want a drink, you can get out," Adam jerks a finger toward the door and needs to recover before jumping a curb, once again.

"At least I'd survive the trip home after."

"Okay, next time we make this trip, you'd better have your licence. I'm not taking this from you when you don't even know how to drive."

"I'm not driving through this part; it's not even lit," Danny notes.

"Come on, Danny," Adam has a cruel smile on his face now and I know something mean is coming, "where's your sense of danger? You're going to be a virgin for life with that attitude."

"Ha-ha. You mean, I'm going to be alive for all the girls I'm having sex with?"

"What girls?"

"Says the guy who hasn't had a date in three years?"

"Because I haven't had time," Adam's a little too quick with the response. "And when they do come, they're going to know I'm tough enough to drive in these conditions."

Jack yawns, "It's fine if you know it."

"Or if you don't have to drive it at night," Adam looks at me judgingly.

It's my turn to be defensive. "What? I don't drive. I didn't think about it."

"All right, that's it, next time you'd better have your licence, too."

"Well then, next time you make the plans," I know he won't and he knows I don't want him to, but it's the threat that matters.

But Adam pulls back, "I was just ribbing you. Honestly, it's not that bad. I mean, there's literally no one around."

"Except you three assholes," Jack murmurs.

"Hey, you can walk too," Adam shoots back, and Danny punctuates it with a

"We probably *should* make him."

"I know the route, I'd catch up," Jack says so casually that I can almost hear the shrug in his voice.

"Not if I speed up."

"You're already ten miles over the speed limit," I note, and the other three just stare at me as if I've said something completely useless and stupid. "I'm just saying…"

"There's no one for miles. I could seriously go one hundred and never even come close to anyone."

"Do it," Jack scoffs. "Gets us home faster."

"I should probably slow down then, just for you."

"Nah, he's just too much of a pussy to go faster," Danny looks to Jack, his child-like blue eyes mischievous, a tiny hint of a smile forming on his youthful lips.

I can't see Jack, but knowing him, he's definitely sharing the scheming look, probably running his fingers slowly through his semi-long brown hair, as though it will somehow pull the ideas out of his head.

"You're right," Jack finally agrees. "He's probably scared to do it."

"It's not about fear…" Adam starts, but Danny cuts him off.

"Too dangerous for you?"

"I'll do it…"

"You probably shouldn't…" I start, but he's already speeding up. Seventy-five…eighty…he's starting to take the curves with speed, as well, flying around blindly on the mostly invisible street.

"He's not going to do it," Danny shakes his head, but this time I don't think he's needling—it was all fun when it was a joke, but he's doubting whether it was a good idea to tempt him.

"Oh, I'm going to do it," Adam's grinning now, totally aware that he's won the game, basically waiting for them to cry 'uncle' and beg him to slow down. But that would be too easy, so the boys in the back keep their mouths shut, just waiting for him to give up on this stupid game.

"I'm trying not to die here," I attempt, but I'm getting drowned out by the revving of the engine. Eighty-five…ninety…ninety-five…

It's like he's on autopilot, barely paying attention to the road, his focus entirely on the speedometer. At this point, I'm half-hoping that a cop will appear from out of the trees and pull us over, just to end this game. One-hundred…one-hundred-five…

"Okay, okay!" Danny's leaned forward to look over Adam's shoulder at the gauge. "You've made your point. Slow down."

And without hesitation, the foot loosens on the gas pedal and the numbers start to drop. One-hundred…ninety-five…ninety…eighty-five. The other two passengers and I breathe a sigh of relief into heavy air. "Told you I'd do it," the smile still hasn't disappeared for Adam. Eighty…seventy-five…

"You shouldn't have done that," I shake my head, annoyed.

"It's fine, nothing happened, just like I said it wouldn't," he glances at me as if to say, *Why are you harping on this*.

And that's when we all hear a thud.

Or maybe it's more accurate to say that we feel it, sending a jolt through the vehicle and into all of our appendages. The car screeches to a halt but our hearts are left fifty feet behind. Everything is so dark.

Adam

Everything feels like it's happening in an order that doesn't make sense—like, I'm pretty sure I had the door open before the car even stopped skidding, and it definitely feels like I got out here while the headlights were facing forward, but they're definitely pointed toward the side of the road now, and there's no way it spun around after I got out. The things in my head haven't been going in order either. I really feel like I yelled out "Oh my God!" after I saw for sure what had happened, but I still haven't fully processed what's in front of me, so it just can't be possible. It feels like I've been standing out here for at least ten minutes, looking on at the dark road and what it's thrown at me, but none of my friends have even fully gotten out of the car yet.

When they finally reach me, they're silent. It's not a cold night; in fact, it's a warm midsummer evening—so why does it feel like all my bones have frozen so I can't even bend my fingers. At some point, I remember that I'm supposed to breathe, but that doesn't make it any easier to do so. It's still not fully sinking in, what I'm looking at, and I can blame the darkness all I want, but in the end, I think it's that my brain just doesn't want to process it.

Then, suddenly, Danny's voice from my left wakes me up, "No. No! Nononononononononononono!!!!!"

"Oh my God. Oh my *God*!" Whatever air is left in me comes out and sucks me dry. No amount of squinting or head tilting is going to change what's there. It's not the lack of light playing a trick on us. It's not a fallen branch or a wind-blown rock. It's a human woman, lying on the ground, one-hundred percent dead.

At least, she's not moving at all. I don't see breathing, no sign of a groan. Even from what feels like a mile away, I know; maybe it's just the catastrophist side of me, but something in the air screams death. Her limbs are crooked and one leg and one arm are definitely shattered. It's hard to see blood in the dark, especially with the dark greenish dress she's wearing, but it looks as though there's a puddle of some kind on the ground next to her. Her face is away from us and the thought of looking at it is dragging my stomach down and completely out of my body, but something tells me that I need to see it.

I've only taken two steps when a hand on my shoulder stops me. It's this little bit of human contact that suddenly makes it all real, like somehow I'm feeling exactly what she can't anymore. "Ambulance!" It feels futile, but it's the first thing that comes out of my mouth. "We need to call!" I'm fumbling in my pocket now, searching for my phone. A familiar act that normally takes two seconds now feels like it's taking forever. These jeans are too tight; my hand is too sweaty. Finally, I've got it out, cracked screen scratching at my fingers as I try to mash in the passcode. Before I can, Melanie's voice comes from the other side of the victim.

"I…I think she's dead."

Even though it had seemed so obvious, my fingers still spasm and the phone nearly drops out of my hand before I catch it and press it against my chest.

"No! No! This is our fault! *All* our fault!" Danny's losing his mind next to me and I'm almost starting to feel sane by comparison. I'm definitely not, though. "Call! Call now! Call 9-1-1!"

I return to fumbling with my mangled screen while he, too, takes his phone from his pocket. "It's dead!" he mourns over his phone battery before catching himself and freezing up at the thought of what he's just said. In shock, he stumbles backward until he's resting motionlessly against the car.

"I'm gonna call, I'm gonna call," I'm trying to reassure him and myself at the same time. Melanie is still looking down at the body, taking it all in calmly, but frozen all the same. I've finally gotten through the lock screen when a stable, controlled hand reaches into my grip and removes the device from my fingers. "Hey! What the hell are you doing? Give that back! We need to call 9-1-1! Now!"

But Jack simply pockets the phone and raises a hand to slow me. I reach for his pocket, but he takes an easy step backward while holding out an arm to dissuade further attempts.

"You're not thinking straight," he says in a tone that's much too level for the situation. He seems totally unfazed, looking at me with a hard, dominant expression that seems much too mature for the soft, youthful face that delivers it. His dark brown eyes bore into me and, even in this darkness, they seem to glow forcefully.

With a swallow, I say slowly, and as calmly as I can muster, "We need to call now. We might not have much time."

Jack is unmoved. "We don't have any time."

"Exactly, so we have to call now," I'm becoming slightly more frantic and frustration is mixing its way in.

"You're not getting it. It's too late."

"We don't know that."

"Melanie. Is she dead?"

Melanie takes a moment, her mouth clicking with dryness as she attempts to wet her tongue before breathing, "She looks pretty dead."

"Put your hand in front of her nose. Is she breathing?"

"I…I don't know; I can't tell. I don't think so…I'm not sure."

Jack clenches his jaw. "You know what breathing feels like. You would know it if you felt it."

Finally, after a pause, Melanie rises, careful not to touch the body, and delivers weakly, "She's not breathing."

"It might not be too late," I insist, my whole body starting to waver, inside and out. I want to charge him and take the phone, just to feel like I'm doing something. I can't understand why he wouldn't even try. I feel like screaming, but at the same time, all of the energy to do it has drained out of me. It's like I'm broken. My words sound hollow, and as though they're coming out of someone else's mouth. "We have to call now."

From the side of the car, Danny is crying. "Just call! Just call!"

Jack holds firm. "What's it going to do?"

"It…"

"No, let me finish." He doesn't snap back at me, he just says it, prodding me into submission. "What's it going to do?" He punctuates each word with a pause, letting them sink in not just for me, but for all of us. "She's dead, we're in the middle of nowhere. It would take an ambulance so long to get out here that there'd be no chance of saving her."

"We have to try."

"All right, and then what happens? The ambulance shows up for her and a police car shows up for you."

"It…it was an accident," I manage dumbly, looking to the lump of human in the middle of the road. And the longer I look at it, the more the curiosity of the situation emerges. "She's in the middle of the road. *She's in the middle of the road.* It's not my fault." In part, my mind eases. It can't be my fault. There's no way I knocked her off the side of the street. Without a doubt, she was either walking in the middle of the asphalt, or she jumped out in front of me. But either way, I'm genuinely innocent.

Any reassurance I might've gotten from that realization is crushed immediately by Jack. "Who cares? All they'll be able to tell is that she was hit with the force of a car driving over the speed limit on a dark and winding street. At best, they don't have enough evidence to pursue the charge and they let you go. But that's low probability."

"Not if we all tell the same story…" I look around at the other two—Danny sobbing, his head buried against the aged grey paint of my sedan, trying to nod in some form of agreement; and Melanie, immobile yet again, trying to process for the first time in a long time a situation where all plans are out the window.

"It won't matter. You were speeding, she got hit. That's all they'll care about."

"But we have to do something."

"We do. But it's not calling an ambulance so that we can go down with her."

"We have to do the right thing."

"Yeah, the right thing for you," Jack takes a step forward to assert further control over the conversation. "Do you know what happens when you get convicted? You killed someone. Even if they go light and call it negligence, it's still jail time and a record. Let's say you get two years—and that's probably wishful thinking—okay, you're still twenty-five when you get out, a lot of life ahead of you. But what kind of life is it going to be? You won't be able to get a good job sitting on that record; a lot of people aren't gonna wanna hang around with a killer. So yeah, you're still young, but you've cut yourself off from a lot of opportunities. This is a life-changer—but really, it's a life-destroyer. All for something that, well, you said it: it's not your fault. So why should you do that to yourself?"

"But…but…what do we do then?" I feel like a child, too dumb to figure anything out for myself, this whole situation still seeming unreal despite the

fact that it's weighing so heavily upon us. Everything he's said makes sense, but right now they're
just horror stories. We need a plan, or something,
anything. My body is shaking again and every
ounce of me wants to run away from this situation,
but then it only gets worse. I'm going to jail. My
life is done. It wasn't my fault. I couldn't have
stopped in time, even going the speed limit. I'm
sure of that.

"We're going to calm down," Jack advises.
"Then we're going to put the body in the backseat
before anyone comes by and sees it, and we're going to take it to a place I know a ways up the street.
Then," he takes a slow, controlled breath, "we burn
it and bury the evidence. No one will ever find it
there and, even if they do, any connection to us will
be destroyed."

"Are you kidding right now?" Danny's looking
at us with terror through his puffed up, boyish face.
"We're calling an ambulance. We have to."

"I'm not going to jail, Danny," my voice is qua-
vering now.

"Do you know how much more trouble you'll be
in—that we'll *all* be in—if they find out we buried
the body?"

"They're not going to find out, Danny," Jack is
firm, bordering on harsh.

"No. This doesn't make any sense. It's bad
enough as it is. Don't make it worse."

"We don't have a choice," Jack reiterates. "Do
you want Adam to go to jail."

"No, but…"

"Then we have to."

Lost, broken, he turns to Melanie. "This is ridiculous, right?"

But Melanie is still wrapped up in silence.

"Right?" Danny prods.

Suddenly, it's as though life has been injected back into her, and her head snaps up, drawing her eyes to make contact with each of us, one-by-one. And with full focus on Danny, she says, "This is his future. We can't destroy that. We have to move fast before anyone sees us."

Danny is clearly stunned. He was certain he'd have her agreement, and now he's simply confused and alone. We all remain in standstill, understanding the gravity of what's about to happen. And then, finally, Melanie declares, "Come on!" and life restarts again.

Jack

"All right, let's get her in the back seat." We've been standing around for too long as it is. At this point, it's a total crapshoot whether anyone comes barrelling along this highway before we have time to get the corpse hidden. Level-headedness isn't running high among any of my friends at the moment, and it's frustrating to be the only one who fully understands the plan. Guess this must be how Melanie feels when we're all bumbling around and missing out on the things she's drawn up for us. Well, maybe not *exactly* the same.

"Stop, what the hell are you doing?!" Adam's made a beeline straight for the body, arms out-stretched, ready to pick her up and throw her over his shoulder. They're really going to need their hands held throughout this thing, aren't they? "Are you trying to get your DNA all over her and her DNA all over you?"

"I thought we were going to dispose of the evi-dence…" Adam seems upset to have been yelled at, and he's clearly not as mentally stable right now as he once was but, as long as he listens, we should be able to get through this. He's usually pretty blasé about things—after all, he is the guy who just drove forty miles over the limit to prove a point. He'll settle down eventually.

"Doesn't mean we have to be careless about it. Get a blanket or something and wrap her up."

"But won't that still put our DNA on her?"

"It's not perfect but nothing's going to be right now. It's better than nothing. Anyway, we'll burn the blanket with her."

As he heads to the trunk, Danny tries to intercept him, to make one final appeal. He's soft—and he's a liability—but we'll worry about that when we have to. Eventually he'll get over it. He's not a lit-tle bitch. He's just acting like one.

"Come on, Adam. You know this is a bad idea. You were ready to call an ambulance, too. You won't go to jail—not if we all tell the same story.

She jumped out in front of the car. You didn't have
time to stop."

Adam's response will be the moment of truth—is
he legitimately dedicated to this plan, or is he a liability as well? "It's too late, Danny. I'm not taking
any chances." Good.

By the way he's looking at the trunk, it feels like
Danny's going to make a lunge for it, to try to block
Adam out. I've always kind of imagined that Adam
has a distinct size advantage on Danny but, looking
at them now, it's really not that much of a difference. Maybe an inch or two, a little more muscle.
It's the confidence versus the slouching that created
the impression. Adam would still win—it just
wouldn't be as easy, or as quick, as it would need to
be. Thankfully, Danny must realise this, and he remains doubled over at the side of the car, allowing
the world to keep spinning around him.

A few seconds later, Adam emerges with a black
airplane blanket and slams the trunk down. It's a
loud and hollow sound that hangs in the still air,
daring someone to have heard it, but there's no one
else in sight. Probably no one else for miles. With
a quick toss, the fabric covers up our dearly de-
parted companion and Adam does everything he can
not to make direct contact with the body. Soon
enough, he has her in an awkward bear hug. Not
the way I would have done it, but I'd rather he mess
it up than that I do it right. I'll help him clean up
his mess, but I won't stick my hands in it.

"Open the door, Danny," I instruct as Adam lumbers in that direction. But he's not moving, looking with fear, sadness, and pathetic pleading at his oncoming friend. We don't have time for this. With three quick strides, I shove the holdout out of the way and open the door myself. Unceremoniously, Adam drops her in the middle of the seat, partly bent, wholly inhuman. "Get in." But Danny simply shakes his head. "Get in or we're leaving you here." He makes one last appeal to the others, but they offer nothing in return. Finally, keeping himself as far away from the body as possible, he slides into the seat.

Adam's already inside, and Melanie and I reach the front passenger door at the same time. "I need to be in the front. I'm navigating." She hesitates but doesn't protest. I'm not sitting next to that thing. I don't care that it's dead, but I do care about keeping my genetic codes as far from her as I can. Behind me, Melanie takes a similar position to Danny's, hugged up against the car door. It's not too long of a drive, but it won't be comfortable for them.

"Okay," Adam starts. "Where am I going?"

"Turn the car back the way you were going and keep on, probably another fifteen, twenty minutes. I'll let you know when we're close."

He nods wordlessly, and this is the beginning of the rest of the trip. For the longest time, nobody says anything, all just considering the position we're in and the consequences that might come.

But there won't be any—not external ones, anyway.
Of that, I'm certain. What they do to themselves on
the inside, that's their problem. One thing's for
sure. Nothing will ever be the same again. Another
thing is: we're stuck with each other, now.

In its own perverse way, I don't mind that. It's
been a long time since I've been stuck with someone I've actually wanted to be stuck with. Even my
mother's barely hung around, making cross-country
trips to visit her boyfriend from the time I was six,
leaving me with my Aunt and Uncle in Chicago, us-
ing family parties as an excuse to get away from
me. These three are going to be stuck with me now.
Maybe not exactly how I wanted it to go, but it
works, all the same.

"We're going to get caught." Apparently, it
doesn't need long to sink in before Danny gets right
back to his previous ways. "This is it. It's too late
for all of us now. We're going to jail." He's sobbing again, and it's a wonder that he hasn't run out
of water yet. His already red and swollen face is
starting to resemble a downy pillow, and he keeps
rubbing at the tears, leaving streaks around his eyes.
"Everything's over for us, now. We're going to die
without ever getting anything we wanted. We've
ruined the rest of our lives already. There's so
much more living and we've already messed it up."

"Shut up, Danny," I mutter, but I don't think he
hears me. Melanie is too tactful to say anything.
Adam, too focussed. It's probably not even worth

it. Might as well let him get it all out and then, hopefully, there won't be anything more to say.

"I'll never get a real job, or…or be able to live my dreams, or make money and…and society will never respect me or anything I do, because I'll always just be that guy—we'll *all* always just be *those guys*—who killed someone. It's over. It's over, and there's no fixing it. It's too late now. I'm…" it's as though something strikes him and even the energy he had to be miserable drains with the shock. "I'm going to die a virgin." Not what I expected to hear and, under different circumstances, I'd probably have made a comment along the lines of *You were going to, anyway*. But no one's in a laughing mood and the joke would be lost in the darkness. "Yeah, that's right—you all know now. I'm a virgin. A twenty-three-year-old virgin. And now, no one will ever want to…I'll never get a chance. I've never known how, and now I'll never get a chance." The crying is overtaking his ability to speak and everything's starting to come out as gibberish, the gist of it being, "It's all over. It's all over."

As annoying as he's being, he's good to have around, usually. It was actually a fairly good week with my Aunt and Uncle, which is more than I can usually say. The fact that the whole "family reunion" trash got canned did a good deal to help with that. I don't know where they get off calling it a family reunion when they do it every year. But having people who actually chose to be with me, instead of just the ones who bat me back and forth and avoid responsibility wherever possible, was a refreshing change.

It probably would've been better in general now that my cousin's gone. He was always greedy and needy, and my Aunt and Uncle doted on him like he was a god. He was thrust on me like a mandatory best friend every time I was forced to visit, and he would take every advantage he could, running off and leaving me to explain his absences, to take the blame because I was older and had to be responsible. As the years passed, it just got worse. He would frame me for his transgressions, lie with a straight face, push me to the brink of sanity. But he isn't around anymore. Always a flighty one, no one's seen him in almost two years, and they've given up on asking. I have to imagine that they only cared at first because they felt like they had to. Just disappeared in the night one day and never came back. Now they're just used to his absence.

I've been lost in myself for a while now and it seems a good time to tune back into reality.

"I can't die like this! There's so much I haven't—I'll never get a chance to—I'm going to DIE ALONE!" it seems Danny's regained his voice, but has yet to find a new or productive idea. A peek by the corner of my headrest shows me that Melanie is deep in thought, staring out the window, trying to ignore her seatmates. Adam, meanwhile, is focussed hard on the road, making the turns carefully, trying to keep to the speed limit despite the vein popping in his forehead that wants him to rush through and get it over with.

"We're almost there," I reassure, if just to keep him alive. If nothing else, I'm glad that I don't have to be the one to drive these roads. It's honestly a miracle he didn't hit more people. There are so many bends and blind turns. The only thing that keeps it from being one of the deadliest stretches in America is the fact that no one uses it. It's too out of the way. The last time I drove it, I nearly went off the road multiple times. This was bound to happen, eventually.

That's not to say it was his fault. There's no way she was on the side of the road when Adam hit her, and part of me is screaming that she jumped in the way. It doesn't matter, though. The second she did it, she settled our fate, but it's not over for us yet.

"Just up here," I indicate a large expanse of field with a small forest in the distance.

"Are you sure?" Adam asks emptily.

"Yep, this is the place."

We still haven't seen anyone around, but that doesn't mean they can't come. Adam pulls up as closely to a cluster of trees as he can before shutting off the ignition. "All right, let's go," Adam says, his door already half-open.

"Hold on." He shuts it again, quickly. "We can't just go dragging a body around out there, looking for somewhere to leave it. Now, I know there are some dirt patches out in the distance that should be good for the burning, but we need to find

a soft spot where we can dig a grave for the bones
and ashes, too.”

“All right, so, let’s go…” Adam flinches toward
the door, again, but stops when he realizes he’s still
the only one who’s moved.

“Someone’s gotta wait with the body and drive
away if anyone gets close.”

“Okay…” Adam nods once, “Guess that means I
have to stay.”

“No,” I shake my head and gesture to Danny.
“Him.”

“What?” Danny’s shocked into reality and it
seems that he must have been listening to us all
along, despite his ravings. “But I can’t drive.”

“Put it in drive. Right one’s go, middle one’s
stop. You’re driving to get away, not to do anything fancy. You’ll figure it out.”

“Leave me,” Melanie volunteers. “I’ll do it.”

“No, we can’t have the guy who’s yelling and
ranting coming with us. If there *is* anyone out there,
there’s no way they don’t notice us.”

“I’ll be quiet…” he doesn’t even sound like he’s
convinced, himself.

“You stay with the body,” I say with finality.
And the other two avoid Danny’s gaze in uncomfortable solidarity. “We’ll be back soon.”

Danny slouches back into his seat and the rest of
us exit swiftly. It shouldn’t take too long now.
We’ve almost made it.

Danny

It's all over—a very tiny part of me is just resigned
to that now, but the rest of me absolutely won't accept it, and that side is winning out. It's a strange
combination, to accept something as unchangeable
history and to need to fight to change it at the same
time. Somehow, I feel like there must be a way out
of this but, at the same time, I know there isn't one.
I want to scream out, like that will release all of the
pent up anxiety and self-destruction inside me and
let me access my mind, to regain the clarity I've lost
over the past half-hour—has it only been half-an-
hour!?—but the fact is that I never had that clarity,
and no amount of wailing will bring it back to me.

I pound my fist hard against the door, barely
even caring that this is Adam's car and he'll kill me
deliberately if I damage it, but all I manage to do is
bruise my knuckles. That pain is a distraction, but
not enough of one. All that keeps flowing through
my brain are the concepts of things that aren't even
real, but that I've lost all the same.

Maybe I haven't done enough to pursue my goals
over my life. Maybe it's largely my own fault that
I'm in this position. Maybe I never would have at-
tained anything. But now, I can't. We'll get
caught—there's no doubt in my mind. Jack might
call this some random hiding place in the middle of
nowhere, but that doesn't mean it's true. There's a
road going right through it, so people have been
here before, and people will be here again,

especially once the sun rises. It may be months, even years, before we're found out, but when it eventually happens, they'll tie it back to us. She's covered in DNA and a date and time of death that put us right there when it happened. I'm trying to convince myself that this is the anxiety talking, but it's not. This is truth.

After that, no one will hire a fugitive, an ex-con, whatever I am at the time. My whole life will be permanently marked. There's always been a part of me that wanted to be something more, greater than just the average citizen, to achieve some degree of celebrity at something—now, that can never happen. If I ever get famous for even a second, it will all crash down as my past is discovered. It's all lost.

And then my personal life will suffer. My family won't want to associate with me. They might put on smiles and say that they're supportive but, when the cameras and judgemental neighbours come out, they'll have *had no idea what he was capable of, the monster*. And aside from the three people here, I will be friendless, except for maybe a few jailbirds who take me in.

Those aren't the kinds of friends I want. I'll be alone. Alone. Alone. Alone. No friends. No job. No…no love. The thought of dying a virgin roils in my stomach. Of course, it's something that's concerned me for a long time, and I've always tried to tell myself not to overthink it, that it would happen naturally when the time was right—but the feeling that I'm overthinking it is dying with each passing second. There's no way of thinking around it now; that possibility has been drained away. I will die loveless, alone, and bereft of that one experience that defines modern human life.

At twenty-three, my life is effectively over. I look to the blanketed figure still seated beside me, as far away as I could get from it, and am struck by the curious kinship. Where my life is figuratively done, hers truly is. I never got a great look at her, but she couldn't have been older than twenty-one or so, still with a full life ahead, so much yet to come—and now nothing will.

I can't stop looking at that blanket, feeling that powerful connection, being drawn to her. Instinctively, I reach forward. I don't know why I do it, but the energy beaming between us, the equal footing that we're both standing on, begs me to solidify that sensation. My hand hovers above the top of the blanket, part of me advising against. But that conscious piece of me died with my hopes and dreams. As the sheet falls aside, her head lolls slightly, facing me with shut eyes and a half-open mouth.

Now, the mental image is complete. Dark hair, full lips, small nose, soft features punctuated by hard cheekbones. She's wearing makeup—not to excess, but enough that it's noticeable. She doesn't look like a person who dressed for the last day of her life. Her dark green dress isn't formal, but it's certainly nice enough that she expected to be seen. Though dead, the energy of life still remains within

her countenance, despite the blood on her hip. It's a
strange thought to think a dead woman is stunningly
beautiful, but I can't keep that out of my head.

I can finally picture her life, all in shades and
blurs, but still living. She had youth and beauty, so
much potential. I can envision family and friends,
parties and tears, love and sadness, smiles and fears.
I can also see everything that she'll never have.
Age, wisdom, strength, all erased in a destroyed future. It's all so real and all so gone and, if my
friends have their way, she'll be gone altogether,
never discovered, entirely decimated. I need to
keep her alive somehow, to preserve her in my
mind.

Her name. That will make her complete, will
give me something to make her more than just a
broken body. There's a hidden pocket at the bottom
of her dress, just above her sleek, white knee.
Slowly, I move my hand there, feeling the pressure
of her flesh pushing against my hand as it slides
along her body and touches her wallet. Slower than
I need to, I remove it, feeling the contact, streaking
across each other, feeling something else that I can't
identify.

Her licence reads Camille Lynn Sheerer, aged
twenty, blue eyes, five foot four. In life, I might
have wanted to know this girl. Camille. I wish I
could bring her back.

As I replace the wallet in her pocket, my hand
draws along her slowly again. It's a feeling I'm trying to fight. I know she's dead. I know it's wrong,

but something inside me is so painfully drawn to her. Soon she will be gone and, with her, every connection. My body is screaming at me, about all the lost things, about this one more thing that will soon be gone.

It's automatic as my other hand slides to the bottom of her dress. Then under it. My stomach freezes as my fingers make contact with the fabric beneath. This is wrong. But something involuntary overrides it and suddenly everything to protect her is volleyed asunder. My own pants are to my ankles and the process has begun before I can stop to think again. The connection is so strong now. I'm simultaneously disgusted with myself and confident that this was necessary. That this was the one thing to keep us both alive as we both die. My sanity rests upon this feeling.

Time disappears and I can't say how long the whole procedure took. But, as I finish, a wash of calm overtakes everything that had blinded me before. For a moment, I rest, eyes closed, nestled into this one thing that still makes sense. Then, for one last time before shrouding her forever, I open my eyes to look at that lost face.

Her eyes are open.

She's staring at me, processing the moment. It's not possible. My heart drops and my whole body goes cold.

"What the hell, Danny?!" a scream of shocked disgust comes from above my head and my eyes shoot up to where Jack is standing. "What's wrong with you?!" He's covering his eyes and looking away while Melanie and Adam stare, perturbed. My glance shoots back to Camille, whose eyes are again closed. But I know what I saw. She seems so dead, but I know better.

Pulling up my pants quickly, I declare, "She's still alive."

"There is literally something wrong with you, man," Jack dares to look again and meets me with absolute revulsion. "You think that would somehow make it better?"

"No, I'm serious. Her eyes were open."

"She's dead, Danny," Melanie shakes her head, still judgemental. "And I think you need some help."

"I think we all need some help," I plead. "Come on, she's still alive. We *need* to call an ambulance, now." The second it's out of my mouth, I realise that it sounds like a made-up excuse to get my way, and I must defend it. "There's no way I'd be making this up after that." So, my perversion is my saviour?

There's a pause as the other three finish processing what they've just witnessed and, finally, Adam breaks the silence. "I think you're delusional." He leaves a long hesitation before carrying on, "But we're all messed up right now. And we do weird things when we're messed up. So, let's just get this over with so we can move on."

Melanie takes a breath and nods once in agreement, her head remaining angled to the ground as she avoids the situation as best as she can. Jack seems unwilling to forget so easily, but time is ticking away, and he eventually succumbs. "Yeah, let's just do this thing. Get her clothes and pick her up."

I'm not sure how serious he is. "Am I going to get some help with that?" Adam takes two steps forward but Jack holds out an arm to block him. Eyes still fixed on me, he clarifies,

"You're the one who just put his DNA everywhere. We're not touching her."

"She was wrapped in Adam's blanket in a car we were all in. It's too late for all of us now."

"Trace amounts versus a big pile of it. You're the prime suspect now. Good job. Now pick her up." He turns away and ushers the other two on ahead before turning his head back to add, "Bring the blanket, too. I'm going to syphon some gas from the tank and then we'll meet you on the other side of the trees."

Trembling, I recover her socks, her shoes, her dress, her panties and pile them on top of her. Once more, I look down at Camille's face, putting my hand on her chest and searching for a heartbeat. I know she was alive, but I can't find vital signs. Maybe my own pounding pulse is drowning out the ability to feel hers. I look from her to my friends and back. There isn't much of a choice. Adding the blanket to the pile, I hoist her up and carefully slide her out of the car.

She's heavier than she looks, and I'm not especially strong, making this journey exceedingly taxing. My knees shake with each step, and the process feels like it's taking most of the night. Finally, we're together at the back edge of the forest, where the three of them have dug a small pit.

"Toss her on," Jack commands coldly. But something holds me back.

"I know she's alive…" I start, pulling her tighter to myself.

"Put her down…"

"No, she's…"

Jack takes three steps forward and knocks into my back. The weight and momentum are too much for me and I start to drop her. The best I can do is keep her from crashing hard to the ground, but that is where she ends up, right in the centre of the pit. Before I can do anything to recover her, face down, articles strewn about, looking so lost and weak, Jack grabs the back of my shirt and yanks me away.

I'm left to watch as he pours the gasoline overtop her, like she's some unseasoned salad. He seems so casual, dripping a little bit here, a little bit there, until she's finally covered. And without waiting or warning, he pulls a lighter from his pocket and sets her aflame.

We all stand in solemn respect for a moment.

But that moment is all it takes before the screaming begins.

From beneath the fire, she wails out, her body twitching in the pain.

"We have to save her!" I cry racing toward the scene, but Jack has me wrapped up tightly. I can only struggle to break free but cannot succeed.

"We have to do something!" Melanie concurs with terror, but Jack shoots her down with a glance.

"It's too late now. She's already gone."

"But we…" she begins but can't find a conclusion.

Weakly, as though he could throw up any second, Adam adds, "Jack's right. It's too late now." Already, the screaming is subsiding and, soon, the only sound is the memory of her wails in our ears. Even still, it takes a long time for the flesh to melt away. If there had been anyone around, we would have been found out by now.

It's nowhere near a hot enough fire to reduce her to ash and, so, as it peters away and leaves what little of her remains on this earth behind, we are left with bone to dispose of.

"All right," Jack says lowly. "Let's cover her over."

"That's not deep enough, though, is it?" Adam notes.

"Do you have a shovel in the car?"

"No…"

"Then this'll have to do."

"But won't she eventually just come back up to the surface…?" Melanie adds.

"If you want to get on your hands and knees and dig, you can go ahead. But no one's ever going to find her here."

Adam and Melanie look at each other, considering their options. Finally, Melanie says, "We'll come back. In a couple of weeks, when no one suspects anything, we'll come back with a shovel, at night, and do this right."

"Fine," Jack allows. "Now, let's get this over with."

The three of them proceed to kick dirt over the bones until the pit is filled. Under different circumstances, they would have frustratedly demanded my assistance, but they know better than to risk it right now. They don't know what I would do. *I* don't know what I would do.

We must be a long way into tomorrow by the time it's all finished, and it's still a lengthy drive home. A lengthy, uncomfortable drive.

Without a word, the other three nod at each other and proceed back through the forest and toward the car. Broken and zombie-like, I follow without thinking. Everything is amplified, from the sound of branches cracking underfoot and the rustling of the branches above our heads, to the feel of the thick, cool summer night air against my skin. I'm paying attention to everything and nothing at the same time. We're well away from the burial site when I trip.

"Watch where you're going," Jack says, tiredly.

The fall has woken me up. It's all real now, but that doesn't seem to matter anymore. With a breath, I start to push myself up when my eyes land upon the thing that felled me. I stop, allowing the sight to process. The others have seen it, too, and the silence amongst us turns from eerie to palpable. On a different day, I would have yanked my foot away and run. But not now. Because the thing that has tripped me is, without a doubt, a dry, blackened, human bone.

Slowly, my face turns to Jack, and Adam and Melanie have done the same. His expression is simple, cold, almost as dead as the things that surround us. He offers no reaction, no justification. He merely allows the moment to settle in and then, finally, he looks to each of us, one by one, and says, "Come on. It's almost daylight."

He proceeds in the direction of the car. And stunned and silent, the rest of us fall in line.

Other Works by Scott R.S. Raphael

A LITTLE SLICE

Emily Dresden was a normal high schooler. Popular, fun, a good student, a kind-hearted person who was looking forward to the future. So, no one can quite figure out why she tried to kill herself last September. Including Emily.

Now back at school after a long recovery, she's cut herself off from her old friends, including her best friend, Daniel, who's determined to help Emily get back to normal. But Emily doesn't think that she can ever be normal again. Not because she doesn't want to be, but because she's convinced that there's something evil inside her, warping her mind and endangering those closest to her. And clawing to get out...

WARNING: A Little Slice contains themes of death, suicide, self-harm, and mental illness, and is recommended for adult readers.

SPRUCE ROAD

The Little Maple Cabin on Spruce Road is the perfect place for an escape from city life. Hidden away in the middle of nowhere, in a forest, along winding roads, it's beautiful, pristine, and quiet. Almost too quiet.

When a group of young friends decides to get away for a birthday celebration, they expect a weekend of drinking, partying, and relaxing by the fire. They don't even have to be careful with their volume, as their closest neighbour—the Cottage's mysterious owner—is two miles down the road. Their closest *living* neighbour, anyway.

When their host warns them of a ghostly presence in the home, most don't take him seriously but, when mysterious things start happening, the group is forced to search for answers...

...and pray that they live long enough to find them...

THE HILL AT THE TOP OF THE MOUNTAIN

Harper Gale is a bestselling author, haunted by the ghost of her recently-deceased husband, and terrorized at work by her disrespectful superior.

Tristan Ames is a rock star, haunted by a dark secret from his past, and terrorized by his bandmates as he struggles to write music again.

Their connection is immediate, but will their personal demons, emotional instability, and fear of moving forward keep them apart?

BEING ON THE ISTHMUS OF RAGE AND DESPAIR

"...being on the isthmus of rage and despair/all I can do is stand, and sit, and stare."

In his debut poetry collection, Scott R.S. Raphael explores the depths of the human mind through a narrator battling the throes of unrequited love, fear, death, fantasy, mental deterioration, and, of course, rage and despair.

An exploration of the human condition and the depths to which one can sink within the darkest corners of the mind, *Being on the Isthmus of Rage and Despair* reaches into what it means to live and seeks the answers sought by many but captured by few.

"*I miss you*/ And I reply,/*I do too*/But I'm not sure if I'm referring to her/or to myself,/for both are equally gone"

About the Author

Scott R.S. Raphael

Scott **R.S.** Raphael is a Canadian author and poet based out of Toronto. He has a B.A. in English and Cinema Studies from the University of Toronto. Raphael has been writing fiction and making art since he was seven years old. He entered the public eye in 2019 when he began posting selections of his poetry on Instagram. Principally an author of fiction, with particular focus upon the horror and fantasy genres, Raphael has written a diverse collection of novels and short stories.

Connect with Scott at:
https://scottrsraphael.com/
Twitter: @scottrsraphael
Instagram: @srsraphael

Excerpt from *A Little Slice*

Prologue

FROM THE WATERFALL of light in the distant hall, the monster came in grey. In many ways, he looked like a man. Head held high and confident, rounded yet angular. Shoulders bony but sculpted; arms long and gangly, but swift. Much swifter than his pace, which was slow and plodding, careful and calculated, cold.

It took a few moments for Elias to realize where he was or why he felt nothing in the haze of darkness around him, eyes drawn to that sterile white light from beyond his captivity. It took a few more to process that he was not going to be able to fight. The monster shut the door behind himself, carefully, making sure to turn the handle to avoid the click.

He was smart, for a monster.

Elias meant to scream but his throat wasn't working. Dry. How long had he been asleep? He might never know.

He might have been dead, already.

In the bed to his left, he heard a boy stir from beyond the curtain. Gasp.

The monster wasted no time with this impediment. His once slow and controlled pace, directed toward Elias's bed, now quickened as he approached the foot of the one that was just beyond Elias's sight. With a violent thwack, the figure sent the boy falling back into a deep, dark unconsciousness that, in the morning, the doctors would attribute to a fall in the night or, perhaps, a lucid dream gone awry.

For now, however, he was out of the way, and the one voice that Elias had left to protect himself against this beast was silenced.

He tried to push himself up in the hospital bed, to back away and disappear through the wall as the monster turned its silhouetted head toward him. He wore some kind of boxy equipment about his entire figure, which glinted in the sharp crescent moon-light that just eked through the window to Elias's right, flickering as trees blew wildly in the way of the only source of light, and smacked against the window with an ominous *clack, clack, clack.*

Returning to his slow pace, the monster approached Elias, as if trying not to wake him, but he soon realized that it was much too late.

Elias yelped, sound finally forcing itself from his throat. But not from fear—from pain. Sharp, shooting pain in his wrists. He looked down and, in the darkness, just managed to pick out the growing circles of blood, beginning to seep through the bandages that held his skin together as the stitches dehisced.

At the sight, his head started to lighten, his stomach loosen, but he had to shake those feelings away. He wasn't one to back down. He'd always been a fighter. Prided himself on it.

So why had he tried to kill himself?

No—that just didn't make sense. It wasn't him. It didn't even feel real. Had it happened at all?

No, he couldn't let himself be owned by that thought now, not when some evil figure from beyond the gates of Hell had burst through his hospital room door and was now reaching his long and dangling arms toward him, flickering in the moonlight, threatening to take him away.

Hands of no use, Elias prayed that his arms still had enough function to save him. He shot forward in the bed, still half-seated upon the hard mattress, swinging wildly at the approaching figure.

A forearm caught his head and the monster stumbled back for a moment, regrouping. Elias willed himself to do the same, but there was only so much he could do from a hospital bed. He fell to his side, tried to right himself upon an elbow. But the figure was charging fast, now.

Elias struck out with a bare foot, pathetic beneath his hospital gown, but enough to buy a few more seconds.

His eyes caught the glint of the window, so near yet unreachable. How far was the drop? It was below the tops of the trees, which was something. But in the darkness, he had no idea just how tall those trees were.

Thinking had been a mistake.

While his brain had been occupied with escape, the monster had prepared his attack, lunging forward nimbly—surprisingly nimbly for a demon of the ancient order—and had latched onto Elias's ankle.

No—not a demon. A man. His eyes shining from behind some kind of reinforced plexiglass suit. In the moonlight, Elias caught flashes of dark, medium-length hair, angular eyebrows, sunken eyes, a hard jawbone sprouting specks of black stubble.

He couldn't have been more than twenty-five, nine or ten years older than Elias, but those eyes had seen a hundred years' worth of horrors. And they threatened to inflict the same upon their soon-to-be-victim.

Elias tried to scream out, once again, as that emotionless, lined face plunged toward him, overtaking his body and stealing whatever power he had left in his heart. A tiny whimper came out, so pathetic that he felt he deserved to be taken. But still, he tried to back kick with his heel as the man engulfed him, ensnared him.

Pain no longer seemed to affect the intruder, as Elias's elbows glanced off the suit, trying to break through it and crush the bone beneath to no avail. He only hurt himself against the hard exoskeleton and felt blood rushing to the surface upon every strike.

As he was wrapped up and lifted, Elias kicked, struggled, tried to slip away but felt himself slipping only into the darkness of unconsciousness as the pain shot through every ripping piece of his flesh and cried out for mercy. "W-what are…you doing?" he finally managed to scrape out of his throat. "Who are you?"

But now was not the time for answers and the kidnapper had no time to waste. He had already taken longer than intended.

The route in had been easy. Empty halls. False scrubs. No one had looked twice on their bleary-eyed rounds. And, if they had, they hadn't acted fast enough.

But soon, surely, one or another would alert security, if not enter this room in the midst of his assault and end the journey before it began. He could not allow for that.

So, as Elias cried out, fought for consciousness, the other man shut off his mind to anything but the present escape, as he drove the two of them straight for the window and slid a baseball bat from a temporary opening in his suit, just above the waistline.

Struggling teenager in one hand and bat in the other, the man smashed the window in one quick motion, barely noticing the shards of sharp glass that threatened their passage, as his suit protected him from all ills.

But Elias noticed, saw the jagged edges stalactiting down toward him, promising to scalp and shave, scar and slice.

And, just as they were about to burst into the night and fall God-knew-how-far, the man finally spoke, in a low, gruff, and cold—so *very, very cold*—voice, "Stop struggling if you don't want to get hurt."

He did. There was no other choice. Elias was weak and he had been overpowered. He shut his

eyes and stopped moving, aside from the shakes that
he could not repel.

He felt the cold night air on his face, cutting
through his skin beneath the sheer gown, his heart
just as cold. And his stomach fell away as they
dropped to the ground. He opened his eyes just in
time to meet the grass below, face planted firmly
into the soil.

But he was alive, he could wriggle his toes. He
could still run, if he could just get up.

The other man was prepared for this possibility—of course, he was, Elias felt stupid for even
thinking that escape might have been an option.
The assailant was already atop him, dragging him
up. His strength was surprising, impressive.

Or maybe Elias was just weak and light from his
self-inflicted anguish. Maybe this was the punish-
ment he faced for having defaced his own body and
invited death into his veins. Even if he knew, despite his actions, that he'd never wanted to die, that
he still couldn't explain why he'd done it.

"If you're going to kill me," Elias began, weakly,
lips barely moving in the winter's cold, "can you
just get it over with?"

Silence—not just from the kidnapper, but from
the world, as they burst into a forest behind the hospital and disappeared into darkness amongst the
trees. He wondered if the man might not have heard
him.

Despite the black, the man seemed to know
where he was going, feet reinserting themselves into

previously entrenched footsteps in the snow. The wind was a terror upon Elias's cheeks, lips, nether regions. But a strange delight upon his arms, so hot and bloody, now beginning to freeze over, numbing the pain away.

They were well out of civilization before the man answered, "You don't want to die. And I have no intention of killing you."

"Oh, no?" Elias tensed, anger starting to overtake him as his fear momentarily dissipated. He tried to turn his neck around to face the figure, but he was too cold; his muscles wouldn't do what he told them to. "Why d'you think I was in there in the first place? Nothing you do can scare me."

If it were possible to hear a smirk, Elias heard it then, as the man slowed his gait and took a much easier pace to the left, down a winding path of trees that seemed, almost, to be a walkway. "Like I said. You don't want to die. I know it. You know it. The only thing you don't know is why you lost control of your body and did something you never wanted to." He laughed slightly and leaned his lips in close to Elias's ear, his breath trapped beneath his suit, but the uncomfortable proximity of his body weighing upon Elias as he neared. "I can tell you that. If you'll listen," he whispered.

"Let me go."

"We're past that, Elias. I came for you. *You*, specifically. I've been watching you. Waiting. I knew you were going to do it. It was just a matter of time." Elias felt cold but it wasn't from the

weather anymore. When it was just an abduction—
he didn't understand, but at least he was prepared
for an out, some blackmail or opportunity to fight.
That hope drained away and left him feeling hollow.

"I was hoping," the man continued, still in his
cold, sinister whisper, "that you'd do it somewhere
more public, so I could access you from the start.
But you just had to do it in your room, didn't you?
You know, I saved your life. I was watching. I saw
it happen and I tried to get in the window to get you
out. Your parents weren't home. You would have
bled out there on your bedroom floor. I watched the
blood pooling around your wrists and seeping into
your hair," he was taking pleasure in the descrip-
tion, in making Elias's stomach turn such that he
would have vomited, if he'd only had the strength to
feel his stomach.

"I smashed the glass, almost got in. But a neighbour saw me and yelled out. I didn't have a choice.
They couldn't know my face or my purpose. I had
to tell them. Tell them what I'd seen, to call for an
ambulance. And while they did that, I disappeared,
still faceless in the night. But I never stopped
watching, Elias. Not when the ambulance came, not
when they took you away, not when they locked
you in that ward. But I was prepared. It's hardly
the first hospital I've broken into and it probably
won't be the last."

They emerged into a clearing around a small
shack, rotted and collapsing, wooden exterior cracking from the vines that snaked through it, from

years of disuse. It looked as though it could col-
lapse at any moment, and Elias had no desire to see
what further horrors it might have held in the light
of day.

"Don't worry," the man smiled crookedly. "We
won't be here long. Just the night. Then I'll take
you away, to a much more secluded location. You
won't have to worry about being found or about
your family."

"I want to see them. Let me go!" Elias whim-
pered.

"No, you don't, Elias. You're a danger to them
now. You may not realize it, but you are. If you
want to protect them, you'll never see them again,
do you understand me?"

"Why?"

"In due time," he dragged Elias across the
threshold and tossed him unceremoniously upon the
scratchy floorboards. He could have sworn he
heard something moving beneath, skittering, squeal-
ing. "Now," he stood over the fallen boy as he lit a
candle, illuminating the fully angular nature of his
young face, "we have a choice. You can be bound
to the bed, taken against your will, and held captive
until I'm done with you. And, believe me, that is
not something that I want.

"Or, you can work with me, Elias. Become one
with my research and embrace the potential that lies
ahead. You can shake my hand and join me. At
least," he espied the bleeding wrist, "you can shake
my hand once I've patched you up." He smiled

again, and it seemed less sinister this time, though Elias could not shake the discomfort he felt from the man's sunken eyes.

The darkness started to overwhelm him. The flicker of the candle hypnotized his gaze as a tiny trickle of smoke began to weave its way past his nose and into his lungs.

"W-what's in it for me?" And, though he couldn't believe he was seriously considering it, he also couldn't help himself. Something in the man's expression, his seriousness. For a monster who had stolen him, he seemed somehow genuine.

"Greatness, Elias. Pure and simple. I—we—this is how we save the world. And everyone will know my—our names." He leaned down closer as Elias started to feel faint from the smoke, felt the night starting to take him away as the blood recommenced its slow drip from his wrists and seeped into the floorboards below. "What do you say, Elias?"

"Who are you?"

He grinned; he sensed victory upon the air as Elias became high with the aroma of the night. "My name is Dr. Ogilvie Thorpe. I am a scientist, a psychologist, a researcher, and a king. But, above all, I am here to save humanity from a darkness that even experts refuse to acknowledge. This is your chance to be a part of my journey. Elias: do you want to save the world?"

And, though he'd already drifted away into a deep and dying sleep, both knew, when he awoke, that his answer would be 'yes.'

Excerpt from *Spruce Road*

1. Nowhere

"You know what the only thing I hate more than bad drivers is?" Mick began in a drole monotone, glancing at Brady, lazed back in the passenger seat, halfway through his second spliff of the drive. "BAD DRIVERS WHO ARE IN MY WAY!" He smacked the horn so quickly it barely blipped.

"Bu-uu-uu-dy," Brady laughed, "calm down." He sucked in deeply and blew the smoke half out the semi-cracked window and half into the face of Gavin, seated behind him and trying not to choke on the fumes.

"I'll calm down," Mick returned to his typical monotone, "when they get out of my…" he jerked the wheel to the right to avoid a braking SUV, "…way."

Gavin grabbed the door for support and still managed to smack his head against the window. Brady hardly seemed to notice the move.

Probably a good thing you don't have to drive behind yourself, Gavin thought, but he wouldn't say it aloud. He didn't know Brady or Mick well enough to offer the jab and, frankly, he wasn't that comfortable with how long they'd been stuck in traffic together. Travis was supposed to have driven him up to the cottage weekend with Alyssa and Mav, but he'd just had to plough his car through a maple tree after a wild night at *Bar Muerte*, leading to a complete reorganization of seating arrangements, and thirteen stitches in the noggin.

"You remember when you used to like driving just for the fun of it?" Brady poked Mick playfully in the shoulder.

"Oh, you mean when I was sixteen and didn't have anywhere to be?"

"And how old are you now? Seventeen? We ain't in no rush."

"Look, just because you're an old man…"

"Guy, I will be an old man when I am thirty, *if* I feel like making it that long," Brady tilted his seat back further, crushing Gavin's knees, but he didn't dare protest.

"What are you, five years older than me?"

Brady just shrugged. "Who knows? Numbers."

"Numbers," Mick concurred as Gavin did some quick mental math, pegging Brady at twenty-eight and Mick at twenty-three, putting him in the middle at twenty-five and a half. And that half mattered. For some reason.

"You missed the turn off," Brady offered uselessly, checking the map on his phone for the first time in fifteen minutes.

"Seriously? Who made you navigator?"

"Not me. Blame backseat," he jabbed a thumb in Gavin's direction.

Gavin raised his arms in mock offense, "I have a name, you know?"

"I'm starting to think we should've let *Gavin navi*gate," Mick chuckled silently at his joke before turning back to dead serious, "now where the hell do I go? We were making record time."

"Look, all I know is, the map said it'd take two hours, and that passed thirty minutes ago."

"Just get me back on track…"

"You just missed a right."

"You didn't tell…ugh, whatever, you know. At least we're having a good time; relaxing Friday afternoon drive up to the country and—SIGNAL, ASSHOLE!"

"Next right, then merge into express," Brady scanned over the turn list. "We're almost there, anyway. Just need to get out of known civilization by about twenty miles, first."

"Why did Kaylyn need to have her birthday weekend in the middle of nowhere, anyway?" Mick glanced at the gas gauge, decided it was full enough to be Sunday's problem.

"Oh, true. Forgot it was Kaylyn's birthday."

"Dude, she invited you. How did you forget that?"

"I dunno, probably high or something."

"What did you think we were going for?"

"Beach, swimming, barbeque burgers, whatever."

Mick glanced over at Brady again, wishing he didn't have to wear sunglasses to combat the setting sun so that his friend and co-worker could see the what's-wrong-with-you look on his face. "It's November."

"Look, it's sixty degrees out, and all I know is, if its fifty-five, you go outside."

"Sixty-five. Maybe."

"Fifty-five. Don't be soft, white boy."

"Soft? Fifty-five is basically a freezer. Gavin, settle it."

Gavin snapped out of his daydream and took a moment to clue in. "Uh, I don't know."

"Cop out, pick one," Mick insisted, and even with the sunglasses on, Gavin could've sworn he saw a threat in the driver's eyes in the rear-view mirror.

"I guess sixty-five…"

"Wait, wait, wait," Brady cut in. "Doesn't count. Gavin works in the kitchen, he's used to the heat." Indeed, Gavin worked in the kitchen at Asher's Palace, where Mick tended bar and Brady served as a sommelier-in-training, rendering them the tightest-knit pair in the restaurant. Truthfully, though, he felt better getting away from the ovens than into them.

"Turn left," Brady instructed, and Mick did.

Then, the world fell away.

From cars and traffic and civilization and people, it was as though they'd broken through a barrier in time and space and come out in the reverse of the universe they'd long known. The road turned dirt and Mick cursed as they bounced violently over a tree root. "I swear, if my muffler's busted, Kaylyn's not getting a birthday present this year."

The trees converged to shroud their journey and when they burst free into barren emptiness a few miles later, the sky had started to turn. "I don't wanna still be driving when it's dark."

"It's cool. Maybe fifteen more miles."

"I'm gunning it," Mick accelerated, blowing through a tiny town of five or seven buildings. His eyes focussed on the road, he could've sworn the woman outside the bank was watching them. Still watching them, a mile past. He tried to shake it off. "How much alcohol'd you guys bring? Should I go back and stop for anything?" He didn't want to go back, but he also felt like he was supposed to, for some reason. That forward was a mistake.

"I'm fully stocked," Brady patted a bag at his feet.

"I'm good," Gavin confirmed. "What happened to getting there ASAP?"

"Yeah, no, just checking. We're still gonna make great time."

They shot back into the forest, Mick turning his hands around the wheel as he curled winding roads at speeds only a local should have been taking.

It would be good to get away, he thought. The restaurant had taken a lot out of him and his tips had to go to something other than schooling. He was never going to do better than bartending, after all. Why keep wasting it all without any fun?

Twilight bit across the sky and a few maple leaves that had stubbornly clung to their branches through the bulk of autumn finally made their dance to the ground around them.

"I've been trying to figure out," Mick said, after an extended silence, "what was—" not *unsettling* or *uncomfortable*—he couldn't use those words even

though they felt right, "—*different* about this place."
He hesitated to listen one more time, to confirm.
"It's quiet. It's *way* too quiet."

"Welcome to the country, my guy."

"Man, I grew up on a farm in the south for the
first ten years of my life. I know quiet. This isn't
that. Out there, there's no sound. Here: it's like
something's eating the sound, if that makes
sense…" he looked to Brady for some kind of con-
firmation and got a shrug. To Gavin. But all he received was a look of shock, a point, and a cry of
"WATCH OUT!"

Mick snapped his neck around just in time to see
a tall, lumbering figure, limping slowly down the
middle of the road, clad all in black. Half-an-hour
later and he would've been invisible if not for the
headlights. Mick whipped the wheel to the left,
sending the back wheels into a tailspin.

Pumping the brakes and tearing at the steering
wheel, he somehow managed to right the car just as
it was about to fly into a ditch at the side of the
road. Heart beating fast, he accelerated as quickly
as he could past the figure, who made no notice of
the fact that he'd nearly been crushed at eighty
miles an hour. Just continued trudging along.

Risking a glance back, Mick tried to make out
the man's face, but in the now-near-blackness, he
could make out little more than a hood and shadow.
"What…" he began, voice cracking slightly before
he coughed and righted himself, "What're you doing in the middle of the road, buddy?"

The others said nothing.

Mick whipped around another corner, deeper into the forest, just wanting the drive to be over.

"Take a right on Spruce Road…I think. My data's cutting in and out."

"There is no right."

"I don't know, take the next right."

"Hold it up or something. Gavin, you have a connection?"

"Nothing," Gavin glanced quickly at the phone he'd been avoiding for the past two hours, anxious as to what his notifications might have brought.

"Great, so we'll just…" and as if a veil had lifted and the world around them had morphed once more, a right turn appeared from between the bushes. Mick made a sharp turn and skidded slightly, knocking the phone from Gavin's hand and leaving him fishing beneath his seat.

In the distance, there was a light. Then two, then three.

And as the car ground to a halt along the gravel driveway that separated a few dozen feet of land from the mass of natural paths around it, the three young men looked up upon a house much vaster and more majestic than they could have imagined.

It was hard to make out much in the dark, but a single streetlight sat outside, to guide the wayward traveller, casting just enough light to let them know that the top and edges of the house were spread so far apart that they disappeared into the darkness.

As Mick turned at a right angle to park next to the car that was already in the drive, the headlights peeled across a rundown post bearing the misnomer "The Little Maple Cabin". Then, like much else, the world was cast into darkness, as Mick shut off the ignition and opened the door upon the new and mysterious realm before them.

2. Preparation

Kaylyn Singh felt like she was going to pass out, but she wasn't going to stop. Not now, not when this was taking forever, as it was. With a deep breath, she closed her eyes, paused, and exhaled with all her might.

The balloon exploded in her hand with an enormous pop that sent the eyes of her boyfriend, Dorian, and her best friend, Mallory, shooting up in shock. "Well, thanks for that!" Mallory rubbed an ear gingerly.

"Are you kidding me? Are you *kidding* me?" Kaylyn exclaimed, jumping up from her seat and aggressively grabbing at the pieces of balloon, depositing them into a nearby trashcan, with violence.

"It's okay, babe," Dorian slid over and placed a hand on the heart of her back, guiding her back to the couches in the middle of the massive living room. "Just sit down and take a breather."

She shuddered his hand off and sat down. Dorian took the hint and kept his distance while Mallory surreptitiously returned to blowing up a balloon of her own. After a moment of silence, Kaylyn settled slightly, though still tense, "I just want it to be perfect. I *need* everything to be perfect."

"Look around you," Dorian soothed, gesturing to the room at large. "Everything's already going perfect."

Kaylyn took another searching glance around the room, taking in the sixty-inch, 4K flat screen; the

six-panel floor-to-ceiling windows that looked out
onto the patio, surrounded by tall, vibrant hedges;
the marble kitchen island, long enough to prepare
three meals on simultaneously; the open footage
that could easily host double, even triple the thirteen
impending guests in this single room, with space to
spare. "I'm really happy with the cottage. I'm really happy with the space," she repeated. "This
is…even better than I expected from the pictures
online."

"See, everything's gonna go fine. It's like that
picture says," Dorian gestured to a photo of a beach,
a motivational message scrawled across the sand,
"'The sand only burns until the flame inside glows
hotter.'"

Kaylyn looked at the photo, blinked.

"Take it down?" Dorian inferred.

"Take it down," Kaylyn agreed.

Mallory finished inflating another balloon and
tossed it into the pile in front of her. "Don't worry,
we're going to get everything done in no time. It'd
be nice if we had a little *help*, though." Her eyes
darted to the staircase down to the basement.

"Whatever, I'm over it," Kaylyn picked up another balloon and started blowing.

"No, they should be up here helping, like the rest
of us."

"I mean, yeah," Kaylyn puffed, "but we knew…"
puff "…what we were getting…" puff "…when we
invited…" puff "…Irina." Kaylyn tied the balloon
off with a wash of relief.

"Why *did* you invite her?" Mallory adjusted her glasses and raised an eyebrow at her best friend.

Kaylyn dropped her voice to a whisper, though she was sure they'd never be able to hear her all the way downstairs in this cavernous place, "I mean, we all like Malachi, and it's kinda hard to invite him and not his girlfriend, especially when we've known her longer."

"So? I mean, we were never *friends* with her, before she started dating Malachi. Now, she just tags along."

"Whatever," Kaylyn had no interest in wasting any more of her precious time dwelling on it. "It's another body to split the cost of the weekend. We'll probably barely see her, anyway."

Mallory collapsed back, starting to unfurl a large "HAPPY BIRTHDAY" poster that was three times the size of her five-foot-nothing frame. "I just wish she wasn't a manager, then we wouldn't have to be nice to her."

"Not like I care, anymore," Kaylyn mused, getting up in search of the best place to hang the poster, now wrapped around Mallory's right leg and left arm as she tried to disentangle herself without tearing the thing to shreds.

"Oh yeah, just keep rubbing it in that you got a big girl job and finally got to quit."

Kaylyn grinned to herself as she scoured the room. Kaylyn Singh, Wedding Planner. It had a nice ring to it. Okay, Kaylyn Singh, *Associate* Wedding Planner. But one thing led to another.

And when her break finally came, she knew that no one would forget her name.

"Oh, you'll get there one day; we all do," Dorian joined Kaylyn in the search, shooting a slightly-irritating-but-probably-well-intentioned smile back at Mallory, now even more entangled than before.

"Okay, but at least you never worked at the Palace that long, Dorian. You were only there— what?—a year?"

"Eight months."

"Eight months. That's barely enough time to have Chef Jorge bust your balls *and* wear them as a necklace. I've been stuck there for seven *years* and am going to die there." The groan in her voice betrayed a much deeper sentiment that no one could miss, but the sardonic tone that she had mastered over the years made it easy to ignore.

"Gotta keep moving. It's not good for me to stay in one place for too long. But anyway, don't worry," Dorian brushed it off, "you don't even have balls to bust. You'll be fine."

"Thanks, Dorian," and she almost sounded like she meant it, although she most certainly did not.

A car door slammed in the distance and the sound was immediately consumed by the night. "Just in time to blow up the last of the balloons!" Kaylyn declared as Mick led a nervous-looking Gavin and a much-too-relaxed Brady into the living room.

"Well, hello to you, too," Mick laughed, removing his sunglasses, which he only now realized he'd never taken off, even in the blackest stretches of the drive. Blinded, yet still able to see.

He shook his head quickly and refocussed on the room, just in time to see a balloon hit him in the nose. Recovering, he batted it back toward Gavin, who was now in the process of attempting to blow up two balloons at once, while still participating in the makeshift game.

"Where the drinks go?" Brady focussed on the important matters.

"Um, the fridge," Kaylyn gestured obviously to the corner of the room.

"Or your stomach," Mick corrected.

"Did I hear the Boozy Boys come in?" Malachi Joseph jogged up the stairs to say hi to the group. In the time since his arrival, the three-hundred-pound teddy bear had changed from jeans into track pants, and he greeted the room with an air hug any three-year-old would've loved to take to bed with them.

"Mister Manager," Brady clapped his hand, and when met with a slightly confused look, clarified. "You shack up with Miss Manager, you become Mister Manager."

"And here I was, thinking I'd gotten a promotion."

"Keep dreaming, busboy," Brady gave him a jab on the arm and offered him a drag on his latest joint.

"Can you do that outside?" Kaylyn waved smoke from her face, though she was nowhere near to the flame.

Brady headed for the back porch. "Not that way," Dorian advised, gesturing to a sign that read *HAZARD: DO NOT USE PORCH!* Brady acknowledged him with a grateful finger gun and headed straight back out the front door.

"Irina coming up?" Mick asked. Mallory covered her mouth to suppress the scoff.

"No, no…" Malachi glanced back downstairs. "She's tired. But she'll be up in a bit. Long night."

"Probably a good time for us to get away, then," Dorian offered, a twinkle in his deep blue eyes. "I know I've needed to get away for a *long* time."

"Yeah, you know," Malachi carried on justifying, "some family troubles, issues with her brother. Guy's kind of a dick. You know how it goes."

"Yeah," Kaylyn smiled kindly, a master of the art of decorum, when she cared to practice. "No rush for her to come up, the party hasn't started yet." She tossed him a balloon, "But now you're here, you can help us get ready."

Malachi glanced down the stairs again, "Yeah, of course," he started to blow, nervously.

Gavin felt a hand upon his shoulder and, a moment later, Mallory had dragged him behind the kitchen island. "Hey, what's up?" he tried to return his close friend's clearly put-on smile.

"Oh, nothing much…good ride up?"

Gavin shot a quick look at Mick and found him engaged in a one-man round of Keep the Balloon Up, well away from the rest of the party. Still, he dropped his voice to a whisper, "Yeah, I mean…I think I might have a concussion, but other than that."

"That good, huh?"

"Yeah, well…" he looked around once more. "I didn't want to say anything because I know Kaylyn was super stressed out with all the planning and driver changes and stuff, but…I'd kinda been hoping to come up with her, you, Travis, or Mav. Would've been a bit more comfortable, for conversation and everything."

"Well, you definitely wouldn't've had to worry about conversation if you'd been with us," Mallory grinned with malice. "Not *your* conversation, necessarily, but *someone* would've been talking the whole way up."

"That bad?"

"I swear," Mallory slammed a hand down on the kitchen island more loudly than intended and looked around to make sure that no one had noticed. She lowered her voice further. "I swear, Irina wouldn't shut up the whole way here. First, she was backseat driving, then she was complaining about the route, the temperature. Then—*then*—she took a forty-five-minute phone call for an argument, in Russian, on speaker phone."

"If it was in Russian, how'd you know she was arguing?" Gavin smirked.

"Oh," Mallory waved her hands dramatically, "no. *She* wasn't arguing. She was *mediating* between two other people on the call who were having an argument with each other. And guess who had to

jack the volume up to freakin' eleven." She paused
to think, "And she kept kicking the back of Dorian's
seat, while he was driving." Mallory raised a hand
to settle the conversation there. "I think that
might've been an accident, but it happened *way* too
often."

"So, I guess I'll take my concussion."

"I *wish* I'd been knocked out for that trip," she
took a deep breath, relieved to finally have that out
of her system.

"All right, all right," Gavin nodded, giving her
time to cool off. "It's all good now. We can finally
relax."

From the door, a loud crash cut through the entire building, booming into the silence around them
with pervasive insistence. Again. And again.
BOOM! BOOM! BOOM!

The room went quiet. Glances were exchanged.
Malachi hiccoughed, grabbed his heart, needed to
sit down. Instinctively, Mick put everyone behind
him, looking to the door defensively.

Unphased, Kaylyn walked past them all and casually moved to the door, as though nothing alarming
or unexpected had occurred. Everyone gathered
around. Everyone but Malachi, still trying to recover his weak heart. Softly, Kaylyn turned the
handle as the wind took the door in and nearly blew
her arm off with it.

Before them, silhouetted in the light of the single
streetlamp, stood a giant of a man. Seven-foot-tall,
hooded, unidentifiable.

But Mick didn't need to look twice to know precisely who stood before them: the figure from the street, the one he'd nearly run down along the dark forested path. The faceless man with no concept of—or maybe, worse, no concern for—the death that came inches from taking him.

Without waiting for an invitation, he took a step across the threshold. And no one would dare ask him to stop. He raised two hands wide enough to crush a neck in a single squeeze and slowly lowered his hood to reveal a hard and haunted face, blanched white and sunken. He may once have been handsome. He may still have been, if not for whatever had possessed his soul.

Slowly, almost creakingly, his lips curled into a taut smile. "Hello," he began in a slow, deep, booming voice. "I'm DJ. Welcome to my cottage."

www.ingramcontent.com/pod-product-compliance
Lightning Source LLC
Chambersburg PA
CBHW030929060726
47591CB00005B/1722